CURVE OF THE DRAGON

CURVE OF THE DRAGON

EPISODE LISTING

CURVE OF THE DRAGON

EPISODE 1 OF 4: CHASING SHADOWS

MATT STOKES

TIME EGG
STUDIOS

Published by Time Egg Studios
Los Angeles, CA
www.timeegg.com

First Edition

Library of Congress Control Number: 2020922207
ISBN - paperback: 978-1-7359509-0-7
ISBN - ebook: 978-1-7359509-4-5

This is a work of fiction. Names, characters, businesses, places, events, locales, and incidents are either the product of the author's imagination or used in a fictitious manner. Any resemblance to actual persons, living or dead, or actual events is purely coincidental.

Cover Illustration: Natalie Shaw
Cover Design: Matt Stokes/Time Egg
Internal Illustration: Ameorry Luo

For Jen and Ed, who have been with me every step of the way. If either of you were ever abducted by a mysterious evil organization, I'd be the first one to come after you.

I mean, try not to have that happen...

But if it did, I'd come bring you home.

CONTENTS

INVOLUNTARY ASSIGNMENT
LOCATION UNKNOWN

RANDALL WOKE up in a room he'd never seen before.

It was a small bedroom, tastefully decorated in grays and earth tones. Streaks of daylight poked through the curtains at the window, giving the room a soft, warm glow.

Still groggy, Randall sat up in the bed to get a better view. There was a small glass desk in the corner, but it was empty except for a notepad. Two chairs were off to the side, turned to face the bed.

Had someone been watching him?

Looking around some more, Randall noticed other little things that didn't make any sense. The picture frames above the bed were bolted to the wall. The bedside lamp was shaped like a strange albino pineapple, which was odd enough that he should have remembered it. The entire room was also spotless, cleaned so well that Randall felt like he'd woken up in a catalogue. It was all very chic.

Randall didn't really do chic.

The only thing he recognized was a freshly pressed charcoal suit hanging on a wall hook near the closet. He had definitely seen that suit before. Was it his? If only he could remember...

Wait. There had been an island. Shouting, fighting, then—

He couldn't remember.

Randall swung off the bed and stumbled to the window, then yanked the curtains apart. Five stories below was a busy street bustling with cars. Pedestrians zoomed along the sidewalk as they went about their day. A few office buildings glinted in the morning sun, framed by small thickets of trees. It was a wonderful view.

He didn't recognize any of it. Where was he?

"Good morning, Randall," said a woman's voice softly in his ear.

Randall jumped, then spun around to look back at the small bedroom.

He was alone.

He could have sworn he'd heard a voice.

"Randall, we have a lot to do today. Please close the curtains and move away from the window."

There was that voice again. How did it know what he was doing? It made his right temple buzz, but it was such a nice, soothing voice.

Randall looked around the room once more, then tugged the curtains closed.

"Very good. It's time to get ready now, Randall. We have work to do."

The woman's voice made his temple buzz again. Was it coming from inside his head? He ran his fingers by his right eye. There was something under the skin at his temple. It was hard, angular. Slightly warm to the touch. What the hell was it?

"Randall, we have a schedule to keep."

"Who are you? Where am I?"

"I'm your doctor, Randall. Don't you remember?"

Right, his doctor. That melodic voice was like warm maple syrup. She was always so good at calming him—

No. His doctor was Gary Flendersen, from back home in Jacksonville. That man would never shut up about his damn boat.

He didn't remember having a female doctor. Who was she?

Randall picked up a card on the nightstand and read the top line: Welcome to the Hampton Glover Park Hotel – Washington, DC.

He was in a hotel. In Washington, DC? He hadn't been to DC since he was a child. Why was he—

This was all wrong.

"You need to get ready, Randall. It's almost time to go."

Randall snatched the suit off the wall and quickly pulled the pants on. Where was his wallet? His phone?

"What are you doing, Randall?"

He didn't answer; his heart was hammering against his chest. Pants were good enough. He had to get out of here. He grabbed the rest of the clothes and bolted for the door.

"Randall?"

Randall fumbled with the lock, his hands starting to shake. He slid the deadbolt open.

"This isn't part of the plan, Randall."

Plan? What plan? Who was this woman?

Randall pulled on the door. It didn't open. How many damn locks did this thing have?

"Randall…"

Undoing the second lock, Randall flung the door open.

"Every part mirrors the whole."

Instantly, Randall froze in the open doorway, clutching his suit. His eyes were blank, like someone had pressed the off switch on his brain.

"We have work to do, Randall. Now please, close the door."

Quietly, Randall reached out and closed the door.

From the back seat of a shiny black town car, Randall watched the trees along Massachusetts Avenue drift by. He caught a glimpse of himself in the rearview mirror and noticed he was wearing a newly pressed charcoal suit. He looked damn good. He was going to make quite an impression on…

Where was he going again?

As the car came to a stop at a traffic light, the driver

turned to look back at him. He had warm, sun-tanned skin, and was somewhere in his thirties. His face was expertly shaven, without even a hint of stubble, and there was a mischievous sparkle in his eye. He flashed a big grin at Randall.

"How ya feeling, buddy?"

Randall thought about it for a moment, then smiled. "Feeling pretty good."

"Good, good. You're gonna do great, Randall."

As the light changed, the town car glided forward once more.

The driver was right, Randall thought. He was going to do great. He felt good. *Ready*. Except for a strange itch at his right temple.

Randall reached up to scratch it and felt a small object underneath the skin: hard, angular, and slightly warm to the touch.

What the hell was that?

"Don't pick at your eyejack," the driver said.

"My what?"

"Eyejack. It's a direct feed to the Doctor. She can see what you see and hear what you say. We've all got one. Makes it easy to communicate."

The driver tapped his right temple, and Randall noticed the slightest bulge near his right eye.

Randall grew uneasy. Why did he have an implant in his head? Why did his driver have one too? Who was this doctor? What was going on? Where was—

Island. Darkness. Pain.

He struggled to remember, but the harder Randall

tried to pull the pieces together, the faster they slipped away.

He tugged the handle on the door, but it didn't respond.

The driver looked in the rearview mirror. "Relax, will ya? We're almost there."

Randall looked up to see an impressive red brick building with the British flag flying in front of it. They drove past it, and turned into a driveway that led to a magnificent English-style country house. At the gate, the driver flashed an ID card at the guards, and they were quickly waved through.

Randall couldn't help staring at the house. "Where are we?"

The driver smiled. "The British Ambassador's Residence. You have a meeting with him today. Don't you remember?"

"Right. Of course." Randall settled back in his seat. The ambassador, that's right. They had a meeting today. An important meeting.

It was for... for...

Why couldn't he remember?

After parking in the roundabout, the driver came over and opened Randall's door so he could get out. He handed Randall a briefcase, then motioned for him to follow.

Randall took a look at it and saw U.S. DIPLOMATIC POUCH stenciled in block lettering on the side.

Moving quickly, the driver led Randall through the complex. They swept through the front gardens, up the elaborate portico, and towards the main entrance. Randall noticed the driver was wearing the same uniform as the guards patrolling the grounds, and had also spontaneously grown an English accent, greeting the sentries at the front door as they passed.

Once inside, the driver made a sharp turn at the ballroom and took Randall to a security checkpoint in the vestibule. An armed guard leaned against a metal detector, while a clerk sat at the security desk arguing with someone on the phone. Randall stared at the clerk for a moment, looking at his ear piercings and the bright streaks of purple in the man's hair.

Randall had never seen purple hair on a man before.

The driver presented his ID card to the guard. "Apologies, we're a bit tardy. Let us through, will you?"

While the guard eyeballed the ID, Randall idly listened to the clerk's conversation. "Sir, I understand you thought your appointment was this morning, but the ambassador has a full schedule, and you aren't on it. You'll have to call back tomorrow when his assistant is here and book something." The clerk hung up the phone.

"Everything okay, Henry?" the guard asked, flipping the driver's ID over.

The clerk sighed. "Yeah, some guy got his dates mixed up and is mad the ambassador can't see him. That's all."

The guard nodded and went back to examining the driver's ID. As he did, the clerk looked over to the driver and they exchanged a nod that was almost invisible.

Seemingly satisfied, the guard handed the driver's ID back. "All right, through the detector with you."

Randall stepped forward, but the driver stopped him and pointed at Randall's briefcase. "I can go through if you want, but he's got a pouch. For the ambassador only."

The guard and the clerk traded a look. They didn't like that answer.

"Don't want to keep the ambassador waiting now, do we?" the driver pushed, harder this time. "Do I need to call someone and chivvy this along?"

The guard eyed the driver and Randall, then begrudgingly waved them through.

With a smile and a nod to the guard, the driver led Randall down the rest of the hallway to a pair of large double doors.

"Doc, we're in position," the driver said under his breath.

Suddenly the Doctor's voice popped into Randall's head again. "Excellent. Randall, please go inside."

The driver opened the door, and Randall stepped into an ornate wood-paneled study. As the door closed behind him, Randall paused to look around the room. The walls were lined with towering bookshelves, which flanked a striking white marble fireplace. Above it hung a portrait of Winston Churchill, who seemed to stare at Randall, questioning his presence.

Across the room, gazing out one of the large Palladian windows, stood the British ambassador. He turned to Randall, greeting him with a wide smile. "Welcome,

welcome!" The ambassador ambled over to Randall and gave him a great clap on the back. "A pleasure to meet you, Randall. Have a seat. Can I get you anything?"

"No, I'm fine," Randall replied, sitting on a plush couch nearby.

As the ambassador went to his desk, the driver's voice piped up in Randall's eyejack. "This is Gecko. I'm at the terminal, Doc. Are we good to go?"

"We are. You may proceed."

A soft click came from the doors around the room. Randall looked back to the ambassador to see if he'd heard it, but he was busy pouring a glass of water.

"The box is locked," said the driver. "Moving to second target."

"Excellent," replied the Doctor. "Randall, it's time to open your briefcase."

That melodic voice was impossible to ignore. Randall put the briefcase on the couch, popped the locks, and looked inside—

Where a cell phone and a 9mm Beretta handgun waited for him.

"Now, Randall, repeat everything I say."

Taking a sip from his glass, the ambassador slid into an armchair near Randall. "So, you're from Gregory's office, yes? What was it you wanted to discuss today?"

Randall paused, listening to the Doctor. Then he pulled the gun out of the case and pointed it at the ambassador's chest. "Fractal has some questions for you, Mr. Ambassador. For your sake, I hope you answer them quickly."

Before the ambassador could respond, alarm bells started shrieking throughout the residence.

Standing on the rooftop of the British Embassy, a Fractal agent watched the ground below, waiting. She was dressed head to toe in tactical gear, with her blonde hair pulled back into a knot. A pair of razor sharp eyes peered out over the half balaclava that covered the lower half of her face. As alarm bells continued to ring below, she watched armed guards race out of the embassy building and toward the Ambassador's Residence next door. She followed every move they made on the ground, quietly noting their numbers, positions, even the formations they grouped into. She could tell by the way they moved and how they entered the residence that they were senior security staff. Well-trained ones.

It wouldn't be long before they reached the ambassador. Her team would have to move quickly.

As the last group of guards entered the residence, she reached up to her right temple and tapped her eyejack. "Scorpion here. I have eyes on the guards, they're rushing the residence. We're ready to move."

The Doctor's voice came over Scorpion's eyejack. "Gecko is bypassing the roof alarms now."

On the roof behind Scorpion were two more Fractal agents, also in tactical gear. The big Samoan to her left, Mastiff, was quietly studying the roof access door in front of him. In his hand was an electric drill, poised over the lock on the door.

The little hairy one, Jackal, kept obsessively playing with his rifle. "When do we get to shoot somebody?"

Scorpion glared at him. "This is a retrieval operation. We're not firing on anyone unless absolutely necessary."

Jackal sneered back. "Ah, you're no fun."

This isn't supposed to be fun, Scorpion thought. When the Doctor had announced the embassy as their target, Scorpion had picked this specific time for a reason. It was a Sunday morning, so the building should be practically empty. Guard presence would be low, especially since most of the on-duty staff was dealing with the Doctor's theatrics in the Ambassador's Residence.

With any luck, they'd get through this without having to kill anyone.

"Alarms are down. You're good to go," Gecko announced over the eyejack. "I'm heading to rendezvous."

Mastiff immediately opened up with the drill, boring through the keyhole on the access door. As soon as the drill chewed through the back of the lock, he removed it and jammed a screwdriver in. He turned it, and the lock clicked.

The door was unlocked. Mastiff gave Scorpion a thumbs-up.

She grabbed the handle and tentatively cracked the door open. No alarm. No cadre of guards. The stairway was clear.

So far, so good.

Scorpion swung the door open and unslung her rifle, checking the suppressor attached to the front. "Moving inside now. Where's the target?"

"Third floor," the Doctor said. "There's a secured office you'll need to take in the northwest corner."

Scorpion's team descended the stairwell and silently entered the third floor. Moving together, they made their way past offices, conference rooms, and through a large bullpen of cubicles.

They were all empty. The place was deserted.

"No one? Really?" Jackal groaned. "What a waste."

Scorpion held a finger up to her lips, and Jackal dropped into sullen silence. They continued along the third floor, past a kitchen and through a lounge area until finally reaching the northwest corner. At the end of the hall was a door guarded by two British soldiers.

Shit, Scorpion thought. She'd hoped to get through this without killing anyone. She signaled Mastiff, who raised his own suppressed rifle. They leaned into the hallway and fired their weapons in unison.

Both guards fell to the floor, each with a bullet hole in their forehead.

The Fractal team converged on the door, with Scorpion and Mastiff taking up positions on either side. Scorpion cracked it open as Mastiff tossed a flashbang grenade into the office. Shouts of surprise inside quickly turned to pain as the grenade went off.

Without warning, Jackal forced his way past Scorpion and into the room. The three British officers inside were still reeling from the grenade, and Jackal opened fire before Scorpion could stop him. He emptied round after round into the room, shooting the helpless men repeatedly until Mastiff yanked the gun away from him.

Jackal squinted at Mastiff, then looked back at Scorpion and shrugged. "What? Doc wanted the room taken." He jerked his head toward the dead officers. "I took it."

Scorpion glared at him and tapped her eyejack. "Doctor, we've reached the office. Where's the Blue Box?"

"Just a moment." The Doctor's voice changed again, becoming more syrupy and melodic. "Randall? Ask the ambassador where the Blue Box is."

Silence. Then after a moment, Randall's voice came over the eyejack. "The Blue Box is a laptop in a case with a red stripe on it."

Scorpion, Mastiff, and Jackal started pulling the office apart. Hidden inside the drawer of one of the desks, Scorpion found a case with a red stripe. Pulling it out, she broke the lock and opened it.

Inside was a laptop.

"Doctor, we've got it." Scorpion took the laptop out, put it on the table, and turned it on. After starting up, the laptop defiantly displayed a password screen. "It's locked. I'll need a password to go any further."

"Let's just take it with us," Jackal said.

"No!" Gecko shouted so loudly over the eyejack that Scorpion and the others winced. "Blue Boxes have a built-in kill switch tied to their GPS. You try to use that laptop in an area it isn't authorized to work in, and it will wipe the hard drive. You're gonna have to copy the files from there."

Scorpion looked at all the dead British officers in the room. "No one here is in any condition to tell us what the password is." Scorpion shot a look at Jackal, who threw his hands up in surrender. "Doctor, we're going to need you to get it."

The Doctor cleared her throat. "Randall..."

Sweat poured down Randall's head as he kept the gun trained on the ambassador.

WHAM!

The doors to the study shuddered as the guards continued to batter them.

WHAM! Part of the left door splintered.

Shouts came from out in the hallway. "Keep it up, they're starting to give way!"

Randall was barely holding it together. He shouldn't be here. He should be back home. Home... in Jacksonville. Wait, that was it! He was from Jacksonville, North Carolina. He should be home with... Haley... and the kids.

Randall panicked as memories came flooding back. He had a family, a wife and three kids. He'd been out of the service for years now, had nothing to do with the army anymore. He owned a carpet cleaning company. They'd just bought a third van.

Why the hell was he holding the British ambassador at gunpoint?

"Randall..."

There it was, that damn voice.

He couldn't let her control him again.

"Randall, I need you to get the password for the Blue Box from the ambassador."

He shook his head. "No, I'm not doing this anymore. I—I just want to go home."

Confused, the ambassador leaned toward Randall. "Who are you talking to?"

More images came flooding back. He'd been kidnapped walking home. There was an island. Fighting, killing, pain, then darkness.

Horrible things had happened there.

"Hey, guys," Gecko broke in over the comms. "I see a group of guards heading toward Scorpion's position. We're running out of time here."

WHAM! The door shook again.

Randall had to get out. Maybe he could jump out the window? It didn't look like that far of a drop.

The Doctor's voice buzzed in his ear, "Randall, listen to me—"

"Get out of my head!" Randall screamed. "Let me out of here, I'm leaving!" Randall was up on his feet, ready to bolt.

"Randall, do you want to see Haley again?"

He froze, scared now. How did the voice know who Haley was?

"Get the password from him, Randall, and I'll set you free."

WHAM! A chunk of wood snapped off the door as Randall struggled with what to do next.

Get the password. Just get the password, and you can leave.

Randall turned back to the ambassador. "They need a password to a—a Blue Box. What is it?"

The ambassador shook his head. "I can't tell you that."

Randall pointed the gun back at the ambassador. "Password. Now."

"I'm sorry, I can't give you that."

The Doctor buzzed in Randall's ear. "Think of Haley, Randall."

WHAM! Another crack at the door.

Randall aimed the gun, and fired. The ambassador screamed, clutching his shoulder.

Screams from out in the hallway. "Shots fired! Shots fired!"

The battering sped up.

WHAM!

WHAM!

WHAM!

WHAM!

Randall couldn't tell the difference between the pounding at the door and his own heart anymore.

Scorpion yelled over the eyejack, "We're under fire! We need that password!"

Randall leveled the gun back at the ambassador. "Password. Now."

The ambassador shook his head, a silent no.

"Randall," came the Doctor's voice again. "Go to the briefcase and get the phone."

Randall pulled himself together long enough to open the briefcase and take out the smartphone. As he picked it up, it began to ring.

"Answer it, Randall."

He swiped the screen to accept the call. A video feed popped up of a small boy laughing on a swing set, being pushed by a middle-aged woman.

"Show it to the ambassador," the Doctor purred.

Randall did as the Doctor said, and the ambassador's face went white.

"That's my boy, my wife," he sputtered, finally getting worked up. "What is this? Are you threatening my family, you little shite?"

Randall and the ambassador watched as the video feed zoomed out to show it was being shot from the window of a nearby building. Next to the camera was a man holding a sniper rifle. He loaded a bullet into the chamber, cocked it, then aimed it at the ambassador's son.

The ambassador collapsed into the armchair.

"The password, Mr. Ambassador."

Tears ran down the ambassador's face. "Through adversity to the stars," he whispered. "All lowercase, no spaces."

"Did you get that?" Randall asked, hoping he was done.

Gunfire popped over the eyejack comms, then Scorpion came back on. "Trying it now."

WHAM! The door to the ambassador's study popped a hinge. It wouldn't be long now.

"It worked!" Scorpion shouted over the comms. "Downloading files to—"

She was cut off by more gunfire.

The ambassador was glued to the phone, the video feed still showing the man pointing a rifle at his son. "I gave you what you wanted." He looked up at Randall. "Please, let them go."

KACRACK! The door to the study finally gave way.

A squad of embassy guards and British soldiers flooded into the room, weapons drawn. They spread out into a ring as a swarm of angry red dots appeared across Randall's torso. The guards all shouted over each other: "Drop the weapon! Hands up! Back away from the ambassador!"

Randall immediately dropped his gun and raised his hands.

Even over the soldiers' shouting, Randall heard Scorpion come back through the eyejack. "Download complete. Heading to exit."

"Good," said the Doctor. "And well done, Randall. You've successfully completed your task. *I release you.*"

A piercing whine rang through Randall's head, dropping him to his knees. He could tell the soldiers around him were shouting, but he couldn't hear them anymore over the blinding pain in his head.

There was something else too. Something hot, burning at the back of his neck. Randall reached back to the base of his skull and felt a small bump that was rapidly growing hotter. It was like his head was on fire. What was—

The small bump on the back of Randall's skull clicked, then exploded, vaporizing the office and everyone in it.

2

HOPE FOR THE FUTURE
NAJAR ESTATE - WASHINGTON, DC

PARTIALLY NESTLED in a grove of trees off of University Terrace, the Najar Estate glittered in the morning sun. Plainclothes guards were peppered around the property, lazily patrolling the grounds for any unwanted visitors.

Out by the pool, a young Egyptian girl reclined on a chaise lounge, casually flicking through various channels on a large outdoor television. "How much longer is this going to take?" she asked as her attention bounced from the TV to the person sitting by her feet.

At the edge of the chaise lounge was a shaggy-haired young man who had barely passed his twenty-fifth birthday. He was dressed simply in a pair of jeans and a plain T-shirt, and stood in stark contrast to the lavish estate. There was a distinct former boy-next-door air about him, one who had grown up into a kind young man.

At his side sat a well-worn kit of mechanical tools, with all manner of wrenches and pliers and other implements poking out. Completely absorbed in his work, the young man was hunched over the Egyptian girl's ankle monitor, assessing his options. He'd pulled apart the outer casing without a problem, but bypassing the tamper alarm was going to be harder than he thought. These new house arrest anklets were getting fancier.

"Hello? Mr. Taylor, can you hear me?"

Amused, the young man looked up at the woman. "Mr. Taylor? I'm barely older than you are. Call me Will."

"Fine. *Will*, when are you going to be done?"

Focusing back on his task, Will rummaged around in his kit and pulled out a pair of tweezers. As he went to pinch a set of wires with them, the girl shifted her leg, shaking the ankle monitor.

Will looked up. "I need you to stop moving."

The girl raised an eyebrow at him. "I need you to answer my question."

"Listen to the boy, Farida," said a deep voice.

They both turned to see the girl's father, Bakari Najar, towering above them in a thick terry cloth pool robe and a vibrant pair of swim trunks. He held out a plate of breakfast kebabs, offering one to his daughter.

"I'm sorry, Baba. I just want to know how much longer I'm going to be stuck here." The girl clicked the channel again, and now angry housewives were battling it out in a posh restaurant. She turned back to Will. "Do I need to start a movie?"

Bakari laughed and offered a kebab to Will.

He politely waved it away, busy following a thin red cable back to its connection on the circuit board. "There you are," he said to himself, satisfied. He looked up at the girl. "Don't move."

Bakari leaned in, looking over Will's shoulder. "What did you find?"

Will pointed to the red cable. "The wire for the tamper alarm. Normally, you'd have to cut it when you cut through the strap on the monitor. Doing that sends a signal to the police, and within a few minutes a group of officers are knocking on your door."

"That would be... unsatisfactory," Bakari said, then bit a chunk of egg off his kebab.

"That's why we aren't going to cut it yet." Will stripped the rubber coating from the red cable. "Engineering is all about studying systems and learning how they work." He took a long wire from his kit and attached it to the parts of the red cable he had just exposed, creating a bypass. "Once you understand what a system was designed to do and how it does it—"

Will cut the alarm cable, but the light on the anklet stayed green. No alarm went off.

He smiled. "You can make it work the way you want." Will slipped the anklet off the girl's leg.

She lifted her foot into the air, admiring her accessory-free ankle. "For all you know, you've just set a dangerous criminal free." The girl looked back at Will, taunting him.

Will laughed. "Your father and I discussed it before I

took this job. If you stop driving around in cars that aren't yours, I think we'll all be fine."

The girl glared at Will, spun off the chaise lounge, and went inside.

It was Bakari's turn to laugh. "Excellent work as always." Reaching into his robe, he pulled out an envelope practically bursting with cash and handed it to Will. "Thank you."

Will took the envelope and dropped it in his kit, then began to put his tools away.

Bakari turned off the television. "Don't be in such a rush. Sit with me a moment. Have a kebab, they're delicious."

"I'm sorry, I can't. I have another appointment after you."

"Five minutes, William," Bakari pushed. He held out a breakfast kebab. "I insist."

Will relented and took the tiny spear of egg, avocado, and cheese.

Bakari sat, motioning for Will to do the same. "Would you ever be interested in more than odd jobs? I could use someone like you on my staff."

"I've already got a full-time job." Will held up his smartphone. "I make chips that go in these little guys."

Bakari thoughtfully munched on the end of his kebab. "And is that what makes you happy? Did you dream of doing this when you were little?"

"It pays the bills."

Finishing his kebab, Bakari grabbed another from the plate. "Life is too short to spend time doing something that just 'pays the bills.' Look around us." Bakari raised his arms, gesturing to the lavish estate. "I did not come to this country and end up with such a house by accident. I worked for it, fought for it, chased it until it was mine. It was something I wanted for my family, for myself, and now I get to lounge by my pool eating the marvelous things my chef makes for me."

Will looked at the two nearby guards and the obvious bulges under their suit jackets. "Surrounded by a dozen of your closest friends with machine guns?"

Bakari followed Will's gaze, then gave a sad smile. "A necessary precaution, considering my line of work. You've done a few jobs for me now, and not once have you mentioned what I do. Tell me, are you too polite to ask, or smart enough that you already know?"

"Can't it be both?"

Flashing a knowing smile, Bakari leaned back in his chair. "Before I moved to the United States, I lived in Cairo. Egypt in the seventies was an interesting place to be a young man. It was a period of great change, conflict, and uncertainty. My father was concerned for our family's safety, and it was during this time that he gave me the greatest piece of advice I've ever received."

Bakari looked directly at Will. "He told me that life comes down to choice, and there's only one choice that truly matters. You either make your own choices, or others will make them for you."

Sighing at the memory, Bakari looked off into the distance. "When your President Carter signed an agreement with Egypt in 1978, my father leapt at it. He chose to move all of us to America. Now I may have a more... flexible relationship with the law than most, but that was a choice I was willing to make. I wanted to build a future for my family, and I've done that."

Bakari pulled another kebab from the plate. "What about you? What is it you want for your future?"

Will shrugged. "To be honest, I'm not sure."

"Why did you choose to become an engineer?"

Will grew quiet, looking down at his reflection in the pool. "I like fixing things, and machines have always made sense to me. When something breaks, you find the part that's causing trouble and replace it. Then everything works again. Good as new."

Bakari leaned forward. "And is everything working in your life?"

Will watched his reflection roll in the water. "People are harder to fix."

"I do not mean to pry, but if you have not found your happiness, you owe it to yourself to go out and chase it." Bakari put a hand on Will's shoulder. "You are still young. But our time is precious, William. Do not waste it letting other people dictate how you spend it."

Will nodded. "Including you?"

"Yes, including me," Bakari said, giving a big belly laugh. "Should you change your mind about the job, give me a call. You will always have a friend here. If you ever need anything, just ask."

"Thanks," Will said, packing up the rest of his tools and closing his kit. He pointed at the ankle monitor still sitting on the chaise lounge. "By the way, that thing needs to keep moving; otherwise, it will look suspicious."

Bakari called one of the guards over, then attached the monitor to his wrist. "Walk around in circles for the rest of the day."

The guard nodded, then started walking around the pool area.

Will shook his head. "Ankle monitors are only accurate up to about fifty feet or so. If you move around inside that, it'll just look like you're standing still."

Bakari considered that for a moment, then called out to the guard. "Make them big circles."

Out on the street, Will popped the trunk of his car as he thumbed through the money in Bakari's envelope. There was an extra thousand dollars that shouldn't be there.

Bakari had overpaid him again.

With an amused sigh, Will tossed the envelope into a box with four more rumpled envelopes filled with cash. *Another eight grand closer*, he thought.

He closed the trunk, got in his car, and headed to his next stop.

Will spent the rest of the morning zigzagging around Washington, trading engineering work for cash. He helped the casino manager at the MGM fix an exploit in his slot machines, broke into a known criminal's computer for the local police, and even rewired a prosthetic arm that had shorted out. In each case, Will ended up with another envelope of cash and the inevitable question: What do you do?

He always answered it, just never the same way. Today, he'd been a microchip manufacturer, a video game engineer, and even the guy who programmed the sounds for car alarms. Will enjoyed coming up with new responses when anyone asked.

He knew better than to give people the real answer.

By the time his last job was over, it was already after five p.m. On his way back to Dupont Circle, Will pulled over at an old convenience store and ducked inside. Behind the front counter was a little boy perched on a stool, watching a stuttering TV.

Will grabbed a water bottle and a bag of chips, then went up to the kid. "Aren't you a little young to be working the counter?"

The kid spun on the stool to face Will. "My dad has me watching the store. He's working on the roof."

Will noticed between the static pops on the TV that the kid was watching a news report. Someone had attacked the British Embassy while he'd been at Bakari's. From the footage, it looked like a bomb had gone off.

"You want to be a reporter when you grow up?" Will asked. When the kid didn't get it, Will pointed at the TV. "Why are you watching this?"

"TV's broken. This is the only channel it gets."

Will looked at the TV. "What if you could watch cartoons instead?"

The kid's eyes doubled in size. "Can you do that?"

"Let's get you some cable."

After a few minutes of work and the highly questionable use of a coaxial cable, Will pulled out of the parking lot as the sounds of Cartoon Network reverberated through the convenience store doorway.

The sun was starting to disappear by the time Will made it to Dupont Circle. Multiple police barricades blocked access to the north as he weaved through a network of embassy buildings and think tanks. After a moment, he realized they were all blocking streets that led toward the British Embassy.

Will continued on, heading east. Finally, he reached his destination: the only building on 19th Street with no logos or prominent signage. It was a plain, unassuming office building with an empty parking lot. The only thing strange about it was there was a guard in the security booth at the main entrance. At six p.m. On a Sunday.

The guard waved to Will as he pulled up. "Beginning to think I wasn't going to see you today."

Will flashed his ID badge. "You know I never miss a Sunday, Oscar."

The guard smiled, buzzing Will through.

After quickly parking his car, Will popped the trunk and pulled a worn backpack over his shoulder. He went straight inside the building, and took the elevator up to the fifth floor.

As the doors opened, Will stepped out into a bare, concrete lobby with no distinguishing features except a giant set of security doors. Will swiped his badge on the card reader. It chirped and displayed in glowing green letters: LOGIN: W. TAYLOR

The magnetic lock on the door clicked, and Will went inside.

Just past the doorway was a massive lobby with TRIDENT DEFENSE SYSTEMS written in huge block lettering behind a reception desk. Large posters lined the walls, showing company executives shaking hands with former presidents and various heads of state alongside giant military hardware. One showed execs drinking beers in lawn chairs on the deck of an aircraft carrier, another had a prominent world leader popping out of a tank wearing aviators and chewing on a cigar. There was even one with a former president in a Stetson sitting on top of a ballistic missile.

Will shook his head as he passed the posters. Normally, a defense contractor like Trident would be the last place he'd choose to work. They didn't seem to have any interest in protecting people or making the world a safer place; all they cared about was increasing revenue for the quarter.

But they had access to satellites, which he desperately needed.

Will headed through the empty lobby, past the offices, and into the deserted cubicle farm. Four rows in, he turned, and stopped at a cube with his name on it. He swiped a picture frame off his desk, then continued past more cubicles to the back of the office.

On the far wall, Will stopped at another security door that read SATCOM. He rooted around in his backpack and pulled out a second security badge. This one had been peeled apart and had an exposed chip stuck to it.

Will swiped it on the card reader. It whirred for a second, then displayed in glowing green letters: LOGIN: ADMIN42739

The security door clicked open, and Will entered a long narrow room filled with workstations on either side. He went down the row, turning on machines one by one until eight monitors were glowing with boot routines.

Picking a station in the middle, Will sat down and propped up the picture frame from his desk. It was a photo of him and a girl who was a few years older, both with the same chestnut brown hair and brown eyes. The girl was tackling Will with a hug from behind as he laughed.

Will smiled at the picture as the machines warmed up, then pulled an envelope from inside his jacket. He turned it over in his hands a few times, playing with the top, where it had already been opened.

He stared at it for a moment, thinking about the letter inside. What it meant.

No. He wasn't going to think about that right now.

The machines were almost ready, and he had work to do.

He slipped the envelope back in his pocket, then looked back at the girl in the picture. "Hey, Laura. Had a pretty good day today, another fifteen thousand toward the trip fund. I've decided to tell Dad tomorrow. Not sure how he's going to take it."

Pulling a binder out of his backpack, Will leafed through it as he continued his conversation with the picture. "I know, but there's been a change, and I don't know that I can wait any longer."

He passed various newspaper clippings about a group of missing American soldiers in the Middle East. He stopped on one for a moment, which had a picture of a young woman in a military dress uniform.

It was the same girl from the picture frame.

CAPTAIN LAURA TAYLOR MIA, PRESUMED DEAD
Capt. Laura Taylor was declared MIA on August 7th, when she and her team disappeared during a mission in Afghanistan...

Will looked back at the picture. "I think I'm your last shot, but I've almost got enough. I'll be there, Laura."

Flipping to the back of the binder, Will opened a section full of maps. There were pages and pages of maps of Afghanistan, all covered with notes. Various areas were circled, with lines, times, dates, and other info.

The machine in front of Will chirped as a SATCOM logo appeared, then transitioned to a detailed satellite map. One by one, the other machines followed, and Will wheeled back and forth on his chair as he pulled up satellite feeds of Kandahar on each computer. He then rolled back to the center console, grabbed his binder, and started taking notes as he studied each of the satellite feeds.

After a few minutes, an IM popped up in the corner of Will's screen.

RED HAT: Candygram.

What the hell? Who would be messaging SATCOM on a Sunday? It couldn't be for him. He wasn't even allowed in this room.

Will decided to ignore it and continue working on the map.

The IM dinged again.

RED HAT: Typically, this is when you'd reply.

Was someone messing with him?

Shit, was someone *here*?

Will jumped up from the console and went back out into the cubicle farm. The lights were still off. No one was there.

Will checked the offices, the conference room, and

anywhere else he could think of. But they were all empty.

He was alone.

Will returned to the SATCOM room and closed the door. He watched another IM pop up.

RED HAT: You still there?

Will hesitated, then grabbed his binder and went to one of the other stations. As he zoomed in on a small camp outside of Kandahar, an IM popped up on his new machine.

RED HAT: Now that's just rude.

Will stopped. He looked around the room. There weren't any cameras. If no one was watching him, then how did the IM follow him to a different machine?

He decided to respond.

SATCOM04: How did you know I switched machines?
RED HAT: I'm watching the server logs to see which machine is receiving active inputs.

Interesting, Will thought. That was pretty smart.

SATCOM04: What do you want?
RED HAT: I wanna help you, Will.

Will rolled away from the keyboard like it had burned him. Whoever this was, they knew his name, and they were talking to him in the SATCOM office he didn't have clearance to be in.

This was five kinds of not good.

Will grabbed his binder and stuffed it into his bag.

RED HAT: Hello, you there?

Not for long, he thought. Will started shutting down the SATCOM machines. He'd powered three of them down when another IM message popped up on all the remaining screens.

RED HAT: Your sister's alive.

Will stared at the blinking IM window, frozen in place.

Then another message popped up.

RED HAT: I can help you find her.

How did they know about that? He hadn't even told his father he was looking for Laura. No one knew.

And yet, here was a blinking IM box, claiming otherwise.

Will slowly sat down and started typing.

SATCOM02: What are you talking about?

RED HAT: I know what you're doing, Will. I can help. I have proof.

SATCOM02: Proof of what?

RED HAT: That Laura's alive. Meet with me. I'll tell you everything I know.

Will was torn. On one hand, meeting some internet stranger who broke into defense contractor networks seemed like a great way to die on a Sunday night.

On the other, they claimed to have information about Laura.

If that was even possibly true...

The IM pinged again before Will could respond.

RED HAT: I get it, you're sitting there deciding if you can trust the internet wacko or not. I want to help you, kid, but time is a bit of an issue here.

If there was even a chance he knew where Laura was...

SATCOM02: When do you want to meet?

RED HAT: Has to be tonight. Is that a yes?

Will typed, then retyped, a response five different times until finally sending—

SATCOM02: Yes.

RED HAT: Good choice, kid.

SATCOM02: Where do I meet you?

RED HAT: Don't worry, I'll find you.

Will tried to respond but got a USER UNKNOWN error in return.

Red Hat was gone.

Sitting back in his chair, Will sighed and stared at the ceiling, still processing what just happened. Who the hell was this, and how did they know so much about him and his sister? None of it made any sense.

Will glanced at his watch. It was just after seven o'clock. Group was at eight, and he didn't want to be late tonight. Whoever Red Hat was, there was nothing Will could do about them until they reached out again.

Will finished shutting down the other SATCOM machines, erased the logs of the IM conversation and his access to the room, then put the picture of Laura in his backpack next to his binder. As he headed for the elevators, he couldn't help wondering who Red Hat was.

And how he knew his sister.

3

HOLDING OUT FOR A HERO
ST. MATTHEW'S CATHEDRAL - WASHINGTON, DC

WILL PARKED his car in front of St. Matthew's Cathedral and checked his watch: 8:15.

Shit. He'd have to sneak in.

Will grabbed his backpack from the car and headed toward the giant medieval building. Out front was a sign that read: Veterans Survivor Group, Sun 8pm–9pm. Will passed it, slipped through the giant wooden double doors, and entered the church.

Despite how many times he'd been here, Will was always impressed by the place. Two long rows of pews ran down the length of the building, split in the middle by a red carpet that stretched all the way up to the altar. On either side, pink marble columns ran high overhead, where they erupted in elaborate stonework as they joined the ornate curved ceiling above. Up at the front, the altar was framed by a huge mosaic of St. Matthew and an angel, surrounded by all sorts of iconography.

Subtle, the place wasn't. As Will took a seat, he wondered if it was possible to be judged by a building.

At the altar, an old man spoke from behind a lectern. "I have my bad days, sure. I still have nightmares sometimes, but things have gotten better. I started an online business with my son. We're selling socks. There's a girl I'm seeing who makes me smile every time I think of her. And most Sundays I go to the lake and feed the ducks, then I get to see you fine people. So, honestly, I can say I'm doing okay."

The man thanked the crowd and stepped down as everyone applauded.

The moderator went up to the lectern as the claps petered out. "Thank you, Carl. Now, who wants to share next?"

Will scanned the crowd. There were only a few dozen people scattered amongst the pews, most of whom Will recognized as regulars. Whoever Red Hat was, it didn't look like he was here.

"Will?"

The moderator had to ask a second time before Will realized the man was speaking to him.

"We haven't heard from you tonight. Did you want to share?"

"Yeah, I do." Will got to his feet. He'd come here for a reason, Red Hat or no. He left his backpack in the pew and went up to the lectern.

It took him a minute to find his voice. "A letter came yesterday. It was a notice from the DPAA, in the crispest, cleanest envelope I've ever seen. If you haven't heard of them, the DPAA is the office inside the military that tracks down missing soldiers. Everyone in this room knows that good news comes by phone. Bad news comes in the mail."

Will pulled the envelope out of his jacket pocket and placed it on the lectern. "It's a weird thing, being scared of an envelope. It took me almost two hours to open it." He slipped the letter out of the envelope and quietly read it to the room. "We regret to inform you that there is no new progress in the search for Capt. Laura Taylor. As it has been a full year since she was listed as missing in action, per protocol, her case will be marked as unsolved. We will update you if any new information arises, but at this time we must move our resources to other cases."

Laying the letter down on the lectern, Will looked out at the crowd. "Reading that was like losing my sister all over again. The worst part is, this letter isn't even for me. It's for my father. I picked his mail up for him yesterday, and when I saw this, I stole it. What's a little mail fraud between family, right?"

Taking a breath, Will continued. "When I was young, we lost my mother, and it almost broke our family. She was the glue that held us together, and for the longest time, I thought I'd never see my father smile again. But slowly, as the years passed, we began to recover. It was just the three of us then: my dad, my sister, and me. When you live through that kind of grief, you don't really heal, you just find a way to spackle over the hole in your heart and keep going."

Will looked back down at the letter. "So I stole this because my dad's hope hangs on the fact that out there, somewhere, people are looking for his daughter. As long as people are searching for Laura, she might come home one day. How am I supposed to take that from him?"

Slipping the letter back into his jacket, Will went on. "Ever since I was little, my big sister has been my hero. She helped me build a treehouse in our backyard. She taught me how to tie my shoes. She explained drifting in *Mario Kart* to me. She even showed me how to throw my first punch, which made sure Billy Dibecki never flipped me upside down at recess ever again."

Staring down at the lectern, Will fought back a wave of tears. "I know that being missing for a full year means Laura's probably dead. I know that. But I also know my sister, and if there's even a chance that someone could survive whatever it is I'm not allowed to know about, then she's out there somewhere. And I'm tired of everyone telling me they can't help anymore."

Will looked back out at the crowd. "A friend of mine told me this morning that the choices we make are what shape our lives, and that there's only one choice that matters in any situation. We either choose to do something, or let others make our choice for us."

Pausing for a moment, Will took a deep breath. "So I've made a choice: I'm going to do something about it. I made a promise to my sister a while ago, and I finally have enough money to make good on it. I think it's a long shot, but I'd never be able to live with myself if I didn't at least try.

"I'd also like to express my gratitude for this group," he continued. "You've helped me so much through this past year, and I just wanted to say thank you. Being able to talk to a group of people who have been through the same thing, who understand what it's like... it's made me feel a little less alone. So thank you."

Will nodded to the moderator, then stepped away from the lectern. As everyone clapped, Will quietly returned to his pew.

There, sitting next to Will's backpack, was a man who hadn't been there before. He was shrouded in a hooded sweatshirt, and the only things visible under it were a stubbled chin and the bill of a baseball cap. He stared straight ahead, not acknowledging Will at all.

Will paused for a moment before slowly sitting down. He pulled his backpack closer to him.

Then, the hoodie spoke. "You ever wonder why church pews are so uncomfortable?"

"Excuse me?"

"Church pews," the hoodie said, shifting a little. "It seems like coming to church every Sunday is already a pain in the ass. Why make it a literal one by forcing you to sit on a plank of wood?" The hoodie shifted again, then gave up on finding a comfortable position. "That was a hell of a speech up there, by the way."

"Thanks."

"If you've got that kind of fire to find your sister, I think you and I have a real shot at pulling this off."

The hoodie turned, revealing the man underneath. He was older than Will, early thirties maybe. It was hard to tell under the stubble and the hoodie. But a pair of hard, alert eyes stared back at him. They shifted constantly: moving from Will, to the aisle, to doing laps around each of the exits. It was like he was trying to watch the entire room at once.

Most importantly, perched on his head was a Houston Rockets cap. A bright red one.

Red Hat.

Will nearly exploded with questions, but Red Hat motioned for him to be quiet. "Not here. We need to go somewhere we can talk."

By now, the moderator was back at the lectern discussing various group business with the room. Red Hat signaled Will to get up, and they both headed down the pew.

As they reached the aisle, three men came through the front door of the cathedral. All of them were dressed suspiciously awful, like they had done a Google search for "how to blend in" and used the first result to govern their fashion choices. The balding one in the flamingo Hawaiian shirt stayed at the door and munched on a soft pretzel, while the two crew cuts dressed like sporty Easter eggs began to move down the rows of pews.

Red Hat immediately sat back down, pulling Will with him. "Okay, new plan. When everyone gets up to leave, I want you to go with them. Wait for me outside."

"You want me to leave? What are you going to do? Who are those guys?"

Red Hat held up his phone and flipped on the front-facing camera. On the screen, Will could see one of the crew cuts getting closer, checking the face of each person he passed. "Look, kid, you have a lot of questions. I get it. If you want any of them answered, I need you to do what I say."

The right crew cut was getting closer. Only a few rows away.

"Okay," Will said. "How are you going to make everyone leave?"

A smile flashed under the hoodie. "Don't worry about that. Just be ready to go."

With that, Red Hat stood up and headed for the front. When he got there, he shoulder-bumped the moderator away from the lectern and took it. "I'd like to share, if that's okay."

Red Hat didn't wait for the moderator to respond. He dropped the hood on his sweatshirt and stared out into the crowd. "Hi, everyone, my name's Carter. Long time listener, first time speaker."

The two crew cuts' heads immediately snapped toward the lectern as everyone else greeted Carter. The crew cuts converged on Carter as the bald man moved up the center aisle.

"It's been a few years since I was last in DC, but I do love hitting the sights when I'm here. This church is pretty famous, did you guys know that? When an archbishop of DC dies, they bury them here. They had Kennedy's funeral up at this altar, right where I'm standing now. It's also the spot where the Supreme Court has their Red Mass each year. What do you think the deal with that is, by the way? Why does the Supreme

Court have a special prayer service? Personally, I think it's because priests and judges shop at the same funny little black gown store, but I digress."

Carter looked at the two crew cuts, who were almost on him. He slowly reached behind his back.

"What I'm trying to say is that this church has seen some crazy shit, but I bet no one's fired a gun in here before."

With that, Carter pulled a handgun and started firing into the ceiling. The entire cathedral broke into a scramble as group members ran for the front door. Will fled with the others, but stopped at the doorway. He lingered just long enough to see Carter golf swing a processional cross into a crew cut's face like it was tee time. Then the moderator and another group member grabbed Will and pulled him through the doors.

Outside, everyone scattered in front of the church as multiple people frantically dialed 911 on their phones. Will stood still on the sidewalk, unsure what to do. Should he go back in and help Carter? How would he even do that? Maybe he should start his car, but what if—

Above Will, a second-floor rectory window exploded into the street as Carter flew through it, using the other crew cut as a battering ram. Spinning in the air, Carter got the crew cut under him and used the man as an airbag as he landed on the ground. Carter stumbled to his feet, shook off some glass, and looked around wildly for a moment.

Then he spotted Will and ran toward him. "You have a car?"

Still stunned, Will nodded.

"Keys, now."

Will gave him the keys. Carter pushed the remote, and Will's car chirped as the doors unlocked. Carter leapt into the driver's seat as Will took the passenger side.

Will stared at Carter. "Did you kill those guys?"

Carter slammed the car into drive. "No, but one of them is going to walk funny for a while."

The car peeled out as Carter tore down Rhode Island Avenue.

"Who were they? Why were they after you?"

The tires squealed as Carter sent the car careening around Scott Circle. "Kid, I know you're about to pop with a hundred questions, but I just rode a grown man through a window. I'm tired. And starving. We're not discussing anything until I get something buried under a pile of bacon. Then you can ask me whatever you want."

Carter poured on the gas, and Will held on to his seat as they rocketed into the night.

One terrifying car ride later, Will was in Silver Spring, sitting in a booth at the Tastee Spoon diner. The place was like a time capsule. Old fifties hits played over the speakers in the ceiling while the few customers thoughtfully munched on chicken fried steaks or sipped milkshakes. People called each other hon and darlin'. It was the kind of place Will would love in any other circumstance.

He'd have to come back when he wasn't on a dinner date with a psychopath.

A stack of untouched hotcakes sat in front of Will, growing increasingly cold. Across the table, Carter shoveled bacon and eggs into his mouth, along with anything else that wasn't nailed down. As he cleared his plate, Carter flagged the waitress down.

"What can I get for you?"

"Spanish omelet for me." Carter looked at Will. "You want anything?"

Will shook his head. The waitress noticed Will's untouched plate.

"Something wrong with your hotcakes, hon?"

"No, no I'm fine."

"Okay, Spanish omelet coming up." The waitress swirled away to the counter.

Carter made another strip of bacon vanish. "You should eat. Always eat when you can."

Will just stared at Carter. "You said you have proof my sister is alive. Start talking."

Carter took a slug from his water glass. "Okay, I've kept you in the dark long enough. Fire away, what do you want to know?"

"Who are you, and how do you know my sister?"

"My name is Carter Callahan. I work in US intelligence. I met your sister when we were both in a division at the CIA."

"The CIA? Wait, you're a *spy*?"

Carter kicked Will under the table. "What are you, five? Keep your voice down, and put your eyes back in your head."

Will lowered his voice. "You said my sister worked with you at the CIA. Are you saying *she* was a spy?"

"Kid, your sister wasn't just a spy, she was the queen badass of Division Six. In other countries, she's the *bogeyman*. They tell ghost stories to new recruits about how Laura Taylor will eat them in their sleep. When someone needs something impossible taken care of, your sister is the one they ask for. She ran circles around most of us, she was that good."

"Better than you?"

"I like to think I held my own."

The waitress reappeared and slid a piping hot Spanish omelet in front of Carter. He handed her his empty plate. "Could I also get a BLT when you have a chance?"

"Sure, darlin'." The waitress disappeared into the kitchen.

Will watched Carter start into the omelet. "How much are you going to eat?"

"Sandwich isn't for me, it's for you. The BLT here is incredible. You'll love it."

"I'm not really hungry."

"For every hotcake you disappear, I'll answer another question."

Will begrudgingly grabbed the syrup dispenser and did a lap over his hotcakes. He cut into one of the fluffy circles, thinking as he ate a chunk. How had Laura kept this a secret from him? From their dad?

"I thought my sister was in the navy," he finally said.

"She was a SEAL."

"She started there, sure, but the agency recruited her pretty soon after that. They like to go around and collect anyone exceptional from the various branches of service. Think of them as the All Star team of the US military."

Will chewed on another hotcake. "So when you say *spy*, did you guys go on secret missions? Travel to exotic locations?"

"Christ, kid. You're talking about James Bond shit. That's usually five to ten percent of intelligence work, tops. Most spy work isn't glamorous. It usually happens in places like this. It's handing off secret documents at a basketball game or meeting with a potential defector at the grocery store. One time, I even toppled a dictatorship from a copy place in Guatemala."

Will pointed at Carter's head. "That how you got your hat?"

"Nah, this is from a Rockets game back home. You wear so many faces in this job, it's nice to keep something around that reminds you of you."

Will sent his fork back to his plate, but only got a

metal clink. He looked down and saw the hotcakes were all gone. Maybe he was hungrier than he thought.

"So tell me," Carter said between forkfuls of omelet. "That speech at the church. You've clearly got some kind of plan, yeah? Let's hear it."

"I know where she was stationed in Kandahar before she disappeared. I've been using the satellite network at Trident to scout the area for a year, and I've mapped every town, trading post, and cave within a fifty-mile radius. I've got enough money to start there, and I'm not going to stop until I find her."

"And what, you're just gonna go knock some heads? Shake the trees until someone gives you a hot tip? It's not exactly the most welcoming vacation destination for Americans, you know. You'd be lucky if you made it a week before a local insurgent cell grabbed you and turned you into a soccer ball."

Will glared at Carter. "You said you could help me. When is that going to start?"

Carter laughed. "First off, I'll save you a trip. Don't go to Afghanistan. Laura's not there anymore."

Before Will could respond, the waitress materialized with a BLT and two new waters. "Someone found their appetite, I see." She set the next round on the table and headed off to help someone at the counter.

Will ignored it. "You know where my sister is?"

Carter pointed at the BLT. "You eat. I'll talk."

Surrendering, Will started in on the sandwich. Carter was right, it was a hell of a BLT.

Carter pulled out his phone. "Do you know when your sister went missing last year?"

"Friday, August 7th, 8:31 p.m. local time in Kandahar."

Carter looked up at Will for a moment. "That's right... down to the minute." He went back to his phone. "The picture I'm going to show you was taken in February, of this year." Carter tapped his phone once more, then handed it to Will. It was a picture of the back of a transport truck, with six people inside it. They were sitting on benches on either side of the truck, chained to a pole in the middle.

The second one on the right was Laura. Her brown hair was chopped short, and she looked like she'd been beaten up. But it was definitely her.

She was alive. Laura really was alive.

Will sat transfixed by the glowing phone as Carter continued. "My sole focus for the last year has been trying to find her, and I've followed her trail all over the globe. They moved her around Afghanistan at first, then I lost track of her. She popped up later in Chicago, then again in Honduras, where that picture was taken. She disappeared for a while after that, but I found her trail again in Malaysia. Currently, I believe she's being held in a facility on an atoll out in the Pacific Ocean."

Will tore himself away from the picture. "Being held? By who? Why?"

Carter stopped and quietly looked around the diner. Then he leaned in and lowered his voice. "Have you ever heard of a group named Fractal?"

Will shook his head.

"I've been investigating them for a while now, and I still only know bits and pieces. They're a clandestine paramilitary organization. Politically, they're completely independent, no official ties to any specific country or government. They're dangerous, well equipped, and available to work for the highest bidder. Their network is enormous, and they seem to have people everywhere. That attack on the British Embassy this morning? Pretty sure that was them."

Will handed the phone back to Carter. "Why did they attack it?"

"I don't know, but my first goal is finding your sister and getting her out. I've tracked her to a base on the Palmyra Atoll out in the middle of the Pacific. The place is a fortress though, and it's too big to search by myself. That's why I came to you. I need your help."

"Why not call in a team from the CIA? Or the military?"

Carter's eyes darted away. "I'm doing this outside the agency. Your sister and her team were NOCs, so as far as the United States is concerned, they had no official reason for doing what they were doing."

"What's a knock?"

"N-O-C, non-official cover. It means the agency won't claim her, even with the evidence I have. Unofficially, I think Fractal has people inside US intelligence, so I don't know who I can trust anymore. That's why I came to you. You're the one person on the planet who wants to find Laura even more than I do, and I think it's safe to say you aren't a Fractal agent. Plus, you have a little military training."

"Four years in the air force. I can handle myself."

Carter laughed so hard he almost choked on his food. "Kid, that should be just enough to keep you from instantly dying where we'd be going. Don't delude yourself into thinking you're ready for any kind of real..."

Carter trailed off, his eyes sweeping the room. "When was the last time you saw another person in here?"

Will looked around. There were no other customers in the place. Hot food was abandoned at multiple tables. Their waitress was nowhere to be seen. Even the cash register was unmanned. When *had* he seen another person? He'd been so wrapped up in what Carter was saying, that he—

"Evening, slugger."

Will and Carter both turned to see the bald man from the cathedral standing in the kitchen doorway, eating out of a pan that lightly dribbled onto his Hawaiian shirt.

Carter recovered quickly. "Hi, Paul. I'd say it was nice to see you, but why lie?"

The bald man, Paul, chuckled. He came up and leaned on the counter like this was a regular Sunday night, then looked at Will. "Who's your date, Carter?"

"Who, this?" Carter asked, motioning to Will. "This is my buddy Dave. We were actually just having a debate about your snazzy ensemble. He thinks you murdered a bunch of flamingos with a silk screen printer just to make that shirt. I, however, kindly explained you were punishing them for eating all your hair."

Paul's grin disappeared as Carter's attention shifted to one of the crew cuts coming in the front door. There was a huge red welt on his face in the shape of a cross, the outline of a tiny savior embedded in his cheek.

Carter gave him a big grin. "Hey, Justin found religion! You can see it all over his face."

"Fuck you, Carter!" shouted the crew cut with the welt on his cheek.

Two more men entered through the side door, one of which waddled strangely as he came inside. Now there were four, including Paul. They all started inching toward Carter and Will.

Carter spoke so low, Will barely heard him. "When I knock baldy down, jump over the counter and get the fire extinguisher."

Will saw the fire extinguisher behind Paul. It might as well have been a mile away.

Paul put his pan down. "Make this easy, Carter. I want to go home and watch SportsCenter."

"Now that's just insulting." Carter reached to the back of the table. "I may be many things, but easy's not one of them."

Carter whipped the syrup dispenser into Paul's face. It shattered, sending Paul screaming to the floor in a sticky mess. Will dove over the counter toward the fire extinguisher as Carter hurled anything he could get his hands on. Dinnerware, napkin dispensers, even the cash register took flight as the men pushed their way forward.

Will held the fire extinguisher up. "Now what?"

"Throw it at New Religion!"

Will chucked the fire extinguisher at the crew cut, and without missing a beat Carter drew his gun and shot it. The extinguisher went off like a bomb, knocking crew cut through the front window.

As Paul got back to his feet, Carter slid over the counter and buried a kick in his doughy gut. Grunting in pain, Paul doubled over and fell back down. Carter whipped a dinner plate into another man's throat, taking him out of the fight. Snatching Paul's pan, he cracked the last attacker in the head until he was too dazed to get back up.

Will looked around in awe. Carter had taken out everyone in the room.

Carter grabbed Will and shoved him into the kitchen, but Paul grabbed Carter's foot before he could follow.

"You son of a bitch, you aren't getting away!"

"Take the hint, Paul. If you want me to go home with you, at least buy me dinner first."

Carter kicked Paul right in the flamingos, then Paul's arm went slack.

Carter ran to the back of the kitchen where Will was crouched, and together they cracked the service door open and looked outside.

No one was visible in the parking lot.

Will tried to go out, but Carter stopped him. "Wait, need to be sure no one's out there."

They waited for a moment, watching. As they did, Will whispered, "Is the bald guy a Fractal agent?"

Carter looked back at the limp Hawaiian shirt behind the counter. "No, I'm pretty sure Paul's just an asshole."

Carter opened the service door further, waiting for an attack, but none came. "If you come with me to find Laura, it's going to be shit like this all the time. I really do need your help, but I'd understand if you said no."

"She's my sister, Carter. When do we leave?"

Carter's face broke into a big grin. "Tonight. Let's get out of here first, then we'll go from there."

Will and Carter squeezed through the door into the back parking lot, then ran for Will's car.

4

LEAD INVESTIGATOR
BRITISH AMBASSADOR'S RESIDENCE - WASHINGTON, DC

WORK LIGHTS ILLUMINATED what was left of the Ambassador's Residence as forensics crews picked their way through the wreckage. Every inch of the building was photographed, catalogued, and scrutinized as investigators whispered theories about what had happened. Some thought a gas line had caught fire, others swore it looked like a drone strike, and that someone in Washington had it out for the ambassador. One particularly salacious rumor involved the ambassador's wife hiring a hitman to blow up her husband for sleeping with one of his assistants.

No matter what their theory was, all the forensics teams kept their voices low and made sure to stay far away from what was left of the ambassador's study. They had been given strict orders that the group inside was not to be disturbed.

Standing in the remains of the ambassador's study, Maia Calderon looked at the floor, thoughtfully chewing on a coffee stirrer. She was in her mid-forties, and exuded a calm, centered confidence that went far beyond the staple gray pantsuit she wore while officially on the clock for the US government. She had a kind face, framed by shoulder-cropped hair in a style that her sister had assured her was incredibly fashionable.

But Maia's most striking feature was her eyes. Brilliant, sparkling, always working. They were two little windows to a supercomputer, carefully studying every inch of the room she was standing in. All around her, scorch marks radiated outward, reaching out like violent fingers in every direction. The southeast wall was completely gone, and the Palladian windows had been replaced by a gaping hole that revealed the driveway below. Looking up, Maia saw that part of the roof had also been destroyed in the blast. She had a clear view of the moon and the stars from where she stood.

Turning her attention back to the floor, Maia looked at the constellation of evidence markers that surrounded her. Each little numbered sign marked a person who had been killed in the explosion. They fanned out in an arc, showing where the British security team had fallen, trying to protect the ambassador.

But Maia's eyes kept coming back to the one evidence marker that was separate from the others, the one right in the center of the scorch marks the bomb had left.

And the mystery man it represented.

Scattered around the office, Maia's team quietly waited as she continued to look around the room, taking in every detail. In more than twenty years with the CIA, Maia had never seen anything like this. She'd encountered her share of bombings, but those had been in war zones, or terror attacks on high profile public targets. They were heartbreaking, but an expected part of the job.

But the residence of a major ambassador? In the heart of Washington?

This was new.

"Play it again, Edgar," Maia finally said.

A curly haired guy in a tie tapped on his laptop. On the large monitor connected to it, a video of the Ambassador's Residence began to play, taken from one of the external security cameras. Maia and the others watched two men who were barely visible through the office window. The fat one was the ambassador, and there was a second man, the one with the gun. Suddenly, a bunch of soldiers rushed the room, surrounding both the ambassador and the gunman. Then the office exploded.

Edgar stopped the video.

Maia looked around the office at the three members of her team. "Okay, room. Our mystery man goes to see the British ambassador, pulls a weapon on him, then explodes. What have you got?"

The Asian woman with the broad shoulders, Lang, leaned against the wall and thoughtfully sipped from her bottle of kombucha tea. "Terrorist attack. He goes in, threatens the ambassador, then gets overwhelmed by the soldiers. Blows his vest. End of story."

Maia spun her coffee stirrer. "No, that doesn't feel right. Why attack the ambassador? It's private, and a strange target."

Edgar shook his head. "No way this is a terror attack. Profile's all wrong. If you want to create terror, people have to see it. Besides, if you were going to attack the UK, why choose their embassy here? Go blow up Trafalgar Square or Big Ben."

Lang took another sip of her tea. "Well, if it wasn't a terror attack, there had to be some goal here. So what was it?"

Edgar looked over at Lang. "Do you have to drink that right now?"

Pausing for a moment, Lang looked at her bottle. *Kom-betcha! Minnesota's Finest* was emblazoned across it in bright green letters. "What's wrong with it?"

"Uh, it smells like dead feet?"

Lang snorted, then took another sip. "Kombucha's good for you. Full of nutrients."

"Wheatgrass is supposed to be good for you too. Doesn't mean I'm going to go outside and start eating the lawn."

"Focus, guys," Maia said, bringing them back. "Our mystery man chose this specific building and the ambassador for a reason. He either wanted something from the ambassador or needed the ambassador to get to something else. Harper, what do we know about our friend so far?"

The girl under the glasses and giant ponytail typed at her laptop for a moment. "Randall Emerson, forty-two, lives in Jacksonville, North Carolina. Married, three kids. Owns a carpet cleaning company. Former soldier, US Army. He was in equipment maintenance and repair."

Maia returned to the video screen. "Edgar, go back to before the soldiers come in."

On the screen, the ambassador's study magically popped together again as the video jumped back, then scrubbed up to Randall pointing the gun at the ambassador.

"Stop." Maia looked at the tiny outline of Randall threatening the ambassador. "Now why on earth is a carpet cleaner from North Carolina waving a gun at a foreign dignitary?"

"He's under duress," said Lang. "No other reason makes sense."

"So he doesn't want to be there, he *has* to be there," offered Edgar.

Harper looked at the video feed. "Then if he doesn't want to be there, someone's forcing him, right? Who's doing that?"

"That," said Maia, still studying the video, "is an excellent question. Edgar, play it again, if you would?"

Edgar restarted the video once more. The team watched Randall and the ambassador argue again. This time, Maia noticed Randall pause before opening the briefcase. Before pulling out the gun. Before pointing it at the ambassador.

He was hesitating.

No, he was *listening*.

Someone was feeding him instructions.

"He's not alone," Maia said. "Someone's talking to him, telling him what to do. Play it again, Edgar. Watch how he hesitates."

The video ran again. Sure enough, the others saw it once they were looking for it.

Lang set down her bottle. "I'll be damned. How'd you even see that?"

Edgar laughed. "That's why she's the boss."

Maia waved at Lang. "Come over here. Be the ambassador for me."

Joining Maia in the blast zone, Lang stood in the ambassador's spot as Maia went to where Randall had been.

"Now, Edgar, slow the video down so we can act it out."

After a few clicks, Edgar started the video again, this time at a quarter of the normal speed. As it played, Maia and Lang mimicked what was on screen, stepping through every movement of Randall and the ambassador. Maia mimed pulling a gun. Lang retreated, fake shouting at Maia. They went through each beat as Maia searched for another clue, something that stood out, didn't fit...

By the time the British guards appeared in the video, Maia copied Randall as he fell to his knees.

Wait a second.

"Pause it there," Maia called out, still kneeling by Randall's evidence marker.

This, this is it. The part that didn't match. She could feel it.

Maia looked up at Lang. "You've seen more field combat than the rest of us. What reasons can you think of that someone would fall to their knees?"

Lang thought for a moment. "Fear, shock, illness, pain. There's a few things that can make a person drop."

"Those are all defensive or reactive. What about aggressive reasons?"

Lang shook her head. "It'd be a major tactical mistake. He was already outnumbered. Falling to his knees would limit his movement options and give the guards better visibility on him."

"That was my thought as well. Can you think of any reason why Randall would fall to his knees?"

"Only that he was afraid of the guards," Lang offered.

Maia shook her head. "He would have done that as soon as they stormed the room. But he didn't. Edgar, look at the end of the video, right before the explosion. Let's see if Randall pauses before he falls to his knees."

Edgar queued the video up and ran it once more.

And there it was. For just a moment after the guards surrounded him—

Randall hesitated, then fell to his knees.

"I don't understand. What does that mean?" Harper asked.

"It means that I don't think Randall fell down on his own," Maia said. "Either someone told him to or made him."

"Made him?" Lang asked. "How?"

"I don't know, but if we assume Randall was here against his will, then someone could have forced him to pull that gun on the ambassador. That same someone then made him fall down after the guards came in, which means—"

"Someone else may have set off his bomb," Lang finished.

"Exactly," Maia said, continuing to chew on her coffee stirrer. "When you put all of those together, it proves Randall wasn't working alone. Harper, search the surrounding area for any communication setup or anything suspicious. Whoever forced Randall into the embassy, they're talking to him. And they can see him."

"On it." Harper went back to her keyboard.

A knock came from behind Maia. She turned to find an aide waiting in the doorway.

"The group from Vauxhall is ready, ma'am."

"Send them in," Maia said.

The aide nodded, then disappeared into the hallway. When she returned, she ushered three UK representatives into the room. The team stood up as Maia greeted each of them. She traded handshakes and polite hellos with the first two, neither of which she'd met before.

The third one, however, she knew all too well. MI6 officer Sebastian George. The man was distractingly handsome, with charisma oozing from his dark skin and bright smile. He was like a smooth rhythm and blues song, wrapped up in a designer three-piece suit that did little to hide the muscles underneath. Combined with his accent, he was dangerously charming. Very gentlemen spy. Even now, Maia could see the aide leering at him like he was a pork chop.

Maia and Sebastian went way back, and the fact that she didn't fall for his charms drove him nuts, which was always fun for her.

She offered him her hand and a warm smile. "Hello, Bash."

He grinned back at her. "It's good to see you, Maiara." Sebastian took Maia's hand and went to kiss it—

But she deftly turned it into a handshake instead. "I wish it was under better circumstances. Let's run you through what we have."

Edgar brought up a map of the Ambassador's Residence, which filled the monitor.

As Maia approached it, her phone rang. She slipped her hand into her pocket and silenced it, then pointed at the center of the map. "Today's attack was focused directly on the ambassador's study, inside the residence. Looking at the size and placement of the blast, the study or something in it seems to be the primary target." Maia looked back at Sebastian. "Aside from the ambassador, was there any target of value worth destroying in this room?"

Sebastian shook his head. "The ambassador's computer perhaps, but that's backed up regularly to the network. Destroying the physical machine wouldn't achieve anything."

Maia waited a moment, watching Sebastian. "Is there any other reason you can think of why the embassy would be attacked?"

Sebastian shook his head again.

"Then for now we'll assume that the ambassador was the primary target, which the footage here seems to support. After identifying the casualties from the attack, we only found one person who didn't match the embassy personnel records you shared with us."

Maia signaled to Edgar, who switched the screen to a breakdown of Randall, including pictures and personal information.

Suddenly, the phones of everyone on Maia's team went off. Maia silenced hers again, but looked over at Lang. Checking her phone, Lang mouthed "CIA" back.

Maia nodded. She'd have to deal with whatever it was after they got out of here.

She went back to the screen. "Randall Emerson, middle-aged carpet cleaner from North Carolina. We believe he was the attacker who detonated the explosive device."

Sebastian looked at the picture of Randall. "Why

would this man want to blow up our ambassador? Do you have any theories?"

"Not anything concrete. Nothing we've found on Mr. Emerson so far suggests he'd have any motive for attacking anyone, much less an ambassador. However, we believe he may not have been working alone. In fact—"

Edgar's laptop beeped as an incoming call popped up on the monitor, replacing Randall's profile. Maia nodded, and Edgar clicked accept.

The pinched face of a man in his early fifties filled the screen. He looked out with a cold, mirthless stare that made him look perpetually annoyed, then squinted at Maia from behind his wire-rimmed glasses. "Ms. Calderon, why aren't you answering your phone?"

"We're going through an intelligence review on the attack this morning. Sebastian, this is Abner Bennett, Deputy Director of Special Operations."

"Nice to meet you, Mr. Bennett," said Sebastian.

Bennett ignored him, focusing on Maia. "We have a Priority One to discuss. I need your team back at Division Six immediately. Briefing in twenty minutes."

Maia couldn't believe it. "Abner, *this* is a Priority One. The British Embassy was attacked."

"And this is a higher Priority One. Briefing. Twenty minutes. I expect you to be here."

Bennett closed the call before Maia could respond.

She looked over at Sebastian and the other UK representatives. "Gentlemen, I apologize. We'll pick this up as soon as we get back."

The two UK reps silently got up and walked out as Sebastian shot a look at Maia that was somewhere between sympathetic and annoyed. Maia mouthed "sorry" in return as Sebastian walked out into the hall.

Maia turned back to her team. "Lang, you're with me. Edgar, Harper, stay here and keep working. We'll cover for you at the briefing."

Edgar looked up from his computer. "Hey, boss? I've been going through the security logs, and an intruder alarm went off a few minutes before the bomb detonated."

Maia shrugged. "That's not surprising. The guards probably sounded the alarm once they knew the ambassador was in danger."

"Not in the residence. The alarm went off in the embassy building next door."

Maia stopped, the wheels in her head turning. Whatever this was, they could only see a piece of it. They needed more.

"I want to know everything you can find out about that alarm. Where it was, who set it off, and why."

"You got it."

Maia nodded, then looked at Lang. "Let's go see what Bennett wants."

They made it halfway to the door before Edgar shouted after them. "Hey!"

Maia and Lang turned back as Edgar pointed at Lang's Kom-betcha! bottle. "Take your nutrients, please. People have to work here."

On the other side of the Potomac in Langley, Virginia, Maia and Lang found the Division Six offices packed. Maia recognized officers from Divisions Four and Five as they all filed into the conference room.

What on earth was going on?

As they grabbed seats, Bennett took up a perch at the front of the room, where he leaned on a podium. Next to him was Paul Mullins, in one of his god-awful Hawaiian shirts. Paul's face was red, and it looked like someone had slapped him around. To Paul's right was another Division Five officer, who had his arm in a sling and a giant welt on his face in the shape of a cross.

Maia couldn't wait to hear what they had to do with Bennett's emergency meeting.

Bennett motioned for quiet. "All right everyone, let's get to it. Until further notice, all of your current projects are suspended."

Surprise vocally rippled through the room, but Bennett ignored it. "As of 0400 this morning, one of the people on our critical threats list popped up in the DC area. I believe many of you will recognize him."

Bennett snapped at a technician sitting at the nearby computer. The tech clicked at his machine, and the briefing room monitor displayed a "wanted" profile.

Carter Callahan's face filled the screen.

The room instantly went silent.

"Carter Callahan. Former Division Six officer, current rogue operative at large. We still aren't sure how he made it into the city, but facial recognition picked him up early this morning in the DC metro area. He has already eluded capture twice tonight," Bennett said, glaring at Paul, "so we're putting everyone on this. Maia Calderon will be running point."

Lang looked at Maia, surprised.

"What about the embassy attack?" Maia called out. "Is looking for Carter really more important than that?"

Bennett glared down his glasses. "We'll get someone on the embassy attack, Ms. Calderon. Don't worry about that anymore. Now, are there any questions?"

The room stayed silent. No one wanted to ask Bennett anything.

"Good, I want action plans on my desk within the hour. Get going."

Everyone got up and shuffled toward the door.

"Ms. Calderon, a moment?"

Now what? Maia stayed as the room emptied. On her way out, Lang said she'd go back to the embassy to help Edgar and Harper. She closed the door behind her, leaving Maia alone with Bennett.

He looked at her coolly. "The embassy attack, get me up to speed. What were you going over with the MI6 officers?"

"We had just started on basics," Maia said. "The attacker has been identified, but the whole thing is strange. He was a civilian, with no motive or ties to the ambassador."

"Anything else?"

Maia hesitated, thinking about the alarm Edgar

found. Her team needed more time to look into it, and Bennett didn't seem like he was in any mood to listen anyway.

She decided to keep it to herself. "No sir, that's it so far."

"All right. Please let MI6 know that we will have someone look into it on our side. I'll see who is free in Division Five."

"Sir, wouldn't it make more sense for my team to do that? We've already started, and it'll take time to get someone else up to speed."

"Then it'll take a little time to catch them up. I want you looking for Carter, Maia. He used to be one of your officers. You're our best bet at catching him."

Seeing that any further argument was pointless, Maia nodded and left the room.

When Maia got back to her office, she found Sebastian sitting at her desk.

"My colleagues stayed at the embassy," said Sebastian, answering Maia's unspoken question. "They weren't thrilled with how we were treated."

"Bash, I'm sorry, but Bennett's on a crusade. There's a special project he's making me head up."

"More important than the attack this morning?"

"Not to me, but my opinion doesn't seem to matter." Maia closed her office door. "Though I don't see why I can't work on both."

Sebastian's eyebrows perked up. "Oh? You want to chase this behind his back? We'd have to be very careful." Sebastian leaned forward. "Sneaking around, secret rendezvous..."

"Turn it off, Bash." Maia waved for him to get out of her chair, then dropped into it herself. "Don't worry about Bennett. I'll handle him if he becomes an issue. Now you, sit."

Sebastian took one of the armchairs across the desk. "Where do we start?"

Maia leaned on her desk. "You level with me. Why do you think the ambassador was attacked today?"

"We don't know yet. We're still looking into it."

"Bash? I don't like it when you hide things."

"I would never."

Maia gave him a hard look. "Oh really? See, I think the attack on the ambassador was theater. A big show to distract us. My team figured out that an alarm inside the embassy was tripped while the attack was going on in the residence. I think whatever was there was the real target. So what was it?"

Sebastian smiled, raising his hands in mock surrender. "I suppose we haven't been *entirely* candid. During the incident at the residence, a team at the embassy was also attacked. The building surveillance was disabled, so we don't know who it was or how many there were. But it was enough to kill two guards and three of my officers."

"Why? What were they after?"

Sebastian grew quiet. "They had a Blue Box with them."

Maia failed to hide her surprise. "Was it taken?"

"No, the Box was still there when we arrived, but it had been tampered with. Many of the files had been copied to a remote drive."

"What was on it, Bash?"

"You know what a Blue Box is, Maiara. Intelligence plans, weapon schematics, troop procedures. We carry many things in it."

They both let that sit in the room for a minute.

"How did you know about the alarm?" Sebastian asked.

"You had a local group in DC install it, which you now know was us. We have monitoring feeds on anything installed in an embassy, especially alarm systems."

"The CIA watches its friends?"

"Especially our friends. It's how we know you're our friends."

Sebastian glared at Maia with a smirk. "Dirty spy."

Maia glared right back. "Cheeky liar."

Sebastian rose to his feet. "I should get back. I need to check in with Whitehall and give them an update."

"Sebastian," Maia called after him. "I will help you find who did this, but you have to be open with me. No more secrets between us, okay?"

"All right, Maiara. No more secrets."

Maia watched Sebastian leave, thinking back to the

embassy attack. How could someone get into an embassy and detonate a bomb without getting caught? Who were these people, and what did they want? Even worse, this didn't feel like an isolated incident. It felt more like the start of something else. If that was true, what was this leading to?

Looking out the window of her office, Maia wondered what she had gotten herself into.

5

BETTER LYING THROUGH CHEMISTRY
PORT OF BALTIMORE - BALTIMORE, MARYLAND

BACK IN HIS CAR, Will sat next to Carter as they looked out at the Port of Baltimore.

Catching a glimpse of himself in the mirror, Will poked at his new hair again. He still wasn't used to it. Carter had chopped it down and dyed it so dark that it almost looked black. Carter had also messed with his eyebrows and forced him to shave.

Will was surprised at how drastically it had changed his appearance. "You think I look different enough?"

Carter kept scanning the docks. "Best I could do with the kinda time we have. I don't think anyone from Fractal is looking for you, but the more we can camouflage you, the better."

Will watched Carter as his eyes flicked back and forth along the different areas of the port. "What are you looking for?"

"Not sure. I'll know when I see it. Let's run through your identity again. Who are you?"

"Will Kirby."

"Who am I?"

"You're Daryl. You're the one who referred me."

"Good," Carter said, still watching the port. "What do you do?"

"I'm an electronics repair tech. I work at a store in DC."

"What about your background? Ever serve in the military?"

Will closed the cover on the mirror and folded the sun visor back up. "I was a private in the army. Got kicked out when I was caught stealing."

"Oh yeah? Why were you stealing things?"

"Army didn't pay me what I was worth. Wanted to balance things out."

Carter nodded. "Good. Stick to that as much as you can."

"Why are we doing this again? Why do I have to lie?"

Carter finally turned away from the windshield and looked at Will. "These guys are pretty particular about the kind of people they'll work with, and this is the only transport that will get us to Palmyra. Trust me, it'll be fine." Carter rummaged around in his pockets, then pulled out a prescription medicine bottle. He popped two pills out of it and handed them to Will. "Take these."

"What are they for?"

Carter paused, taking a second to check the label. "ADHD meds. Just take them."

"I don't have ADHD."

"I know, but they'll spike your metabolism. It's the fastest way to burn through sodium thiopental."

"Sodium what?"

"Truth serum. Boosting your metabolism will make it wear off faster. Having amphetamines and thiopental in your system at the same time is gonna be a roller-coaster though."

"Truth serum? Carter, what the hell are you sending me into?"

Carter looked back out at the port. "It's better if I don't tell you, you'll react more naturally. Just answer their questions and stick to your backstory. You should be fine."

Will didn't know what to say, so he quietly swallowed the pills.

Carter sighed. "Kid, I'm not going to lie. This is the first step in what will probably be a giant chain of dangerous, potentially fatal decisions. You can still turn back if you want, but this is your last chance to bail out."

In one of the warehouses, the lights blinked on, then off. They did it a second time, and a third. Then the warehouse stayed dark.

Carter looked at Will. "Decision time. What's it going to be?"

Will looked at the warehouse. "Let's go find my sister."

The warehouse door slid open as Will approached, and a crusty-looking worker waved him in. Will stepped inside, extremely aware of the large door as it shut and locked behind him.

The crusty worker patted Will down, moving quickly with obvious experience. He relieved Will of his cell phone.

"Am I going to get that back?"

The worker tossed it in a box with multiple other phones. "Sure." He pulled Will over to a small table. "Stand still," he said as he took Will's forearm, cleaned it with an alcohol wipe, then jabbed a hypodermic needle into Will's vein. The needle was connected to a small tube, which ran up into a box of IV bags.

"What's this for?"

The only answer Will got was a glare and more silence as the worker taped the needle down. He picked up the IV bag the tube was connected to and gave it to Will. "Keep the bag high."

Will took the bag in his left hand as the worker got up and walked into the warehouse stacks. He motioned for Will to follow, and Will hurried after him as he clutched his IV bag souvenir.

They walked through rows of shipping crates and containers without saying a word. The trip through the warehouse seemed to go on forever, then Will remembered the drugs. Carter had warned him the amphetamines he'd taken in the car would amp him up.

Focus, he thought. *Just follow this guy to wherever we're going.*

The worker led Will around the corner and down another row of containers, which gradually grew brighter as they approached a room that still had the lights on. When they reached it, the worker motioned for Will to go inside.

The room had been converted into a makeshift office containing a desk and little else. Sitting behind the desk was a small plump of a man in a sweater vest and a bow tie. Wild gray tufts of hair on either side of his head framed his incredibly precise, round spectacles. He looked like some kind of professor or a psychiatrist.

Will wondered what this guy was doing in a shipping warehouse.

The Spectacled Man stood, smiling at Will. "Hello." He motioned to the empty chair at the center of the room. "Please, have a seat."

As Will sat, the entire room went fuzzy for a moment. He was starting to feel a little slower. The drugs in the IV bag must be kicking in.

Truth serum.

This entire thing was insane.

"I'm going to run you through some standard questions," the Spectacled Man said. "Please answer them as best you can."

Will nodded. Whatever was in that bag hit fast.

"What's your name?"

"Will."

"Do you have a last name, Will?"

Wait, what the hell was it. Not Taylor, something else. It was...

"Kirby."

"Okay, Will, what is it you do for a living?" the Spectacled Man asked.

"I-I fix TVs and things." Was that what he did? Will's mind was getting foggy. It was hard to think.

"Do you like your job?"

"Not really. They don't pay me enough."

"Do you feel frustrated at work?"

"Yeah, sometimes."

The Spectacled Man made some notes as Will looked at the bag attached to his arm. Suddenly, he had a spike of clarity. He couldn't think because there were drugs in the bag. He needed to pull the IV out, then he—

He...

Wait, what was he supposed to do? Things were so cloudy, it felt like he was thinking underwater.

"Will?"

Was someone talking to him? He looked up and saw the Spectacled Man. "Yes?"

"How does being frustrated at work effect your home life?"

"It... doesn't really."

"No? Does it upset your wife?"

"Not married."

"Girlfriend? Any family at home?"

"No, I live by myself," Will managed to get out. What

were these questions about? What did they possibly have to do with traveling to Palmyra?

Wait. Will could think again. The bag. The drugs were in the bag. Will shifted the IV bag around so he could pinch the tube and stop the flow of liquid into his arm.

"Let's shift gears a little. Have you ever served in the military?"

"Yes. Air force."

Shit, wait, was that wrong?

"Really? You were in the air force? What did you do?"

Will started to sweat. He had been in the air force. Wasn't that the right answer? No, wait. Carter had told him to say something else. It was, it was—

"No, I was a private. US Army."

The Spectacled Man stopped, studying Will for a moment. "I'm confused, were you in the air force or the army?"

Concentrating hard, Will tried to push back the haze of drugs his brain was swimming in.

"I was... in the army. Sorry, it's hard to think. I feel like I'm drunk..."

A thin smile curled on the Spectacled Man's face. "That's just the medicine in the bag. It ensures we have an open conversation. Just relax, you'll get used to it. Now, did you ever see any combat?"

"No, I was a repair tech." The answers were getting a little easier. The fog was starting to lift.

"What kind of weapons training did you have?"

"Small arms, automatic rifles, standard stuff in basic."

"I see." The Spectacled Man made more notes. "Why did you leave the army?"

"Had to, I was kicked out."

"Oh? For what?"

"I was caught stealing from the equipment stores."

"Why did you do that?"

"They didn't pay me enough. Thought I'd balance things out a little."

Will rolled his head as the amphetamines came back full force. He was getting antsy, but at least he could think again.

"I think you'll enjoy the kind of work we have for you, Mr. Kirby. We'll make sure you get paid what you're worth."

Paid? Was this a job interview? Will checked to make sure the IV tube was still pinched closed. It was.

He looked back up at the Spectacled Man. "Daryl didn't really tell me much about the job. What exactly will I be doing?"

The Spectacled Man put down his notes and walked over to Will. He pulled the IV out of Will's arm, then helped him to his feet. "It's easier to show you. Come with me." He led Will behind his desk and opened a thick sliding door.

Two men the size of grizzly bears were waiting on the other side.

"Mr. Kirby, welcome to Fractal."

Before Will could react, one of the men jabbed a

needle in his neck, shooting a third cocktail into his already overcrowded bloodstream. Will's muscles betrayed him, and he fell to the floor. The other man scooped him up and carried him into the back of the warehouse. Still conscious, Will saw more men shoveling limp bodies into black vans that disappeared as soon as they were full.

The man carrying Will dumped him in a pile next to a few other victims, each as paralyzed as he was. One by one they disappeared as they were taken away to the vans.

Then one of the men loading the vans came for him. He looked familiar, which Will thought was strange. He didn't know any van kidnappers that he could think of.

As the man picked him up, Will got a good look at his face.

It was Carter.

Will tried to scream, fight back, but whatever he'd been injected with had turned him into a lump that couldn't do any of those things. Will stared at Carter as he carried him across the loading area and threw him in the back of a van. Carter's eyes briefly met Will's, then he slammed the van door shut.

As the van pulled away, the last of Will's resistance faded, and he passed out.

6

SURPRISE LANDING

TWENTY-YEAR-OLD WILL TAYLOR slammed into the ground face first, taking in a generous mouthful of dirt. From somewhere above him came infectious laughter. "C'mon, I taught you better than that."

A hand appeared above Will, ready to help. He took it and pulled himself back to his feet.

Standing in front of him was his sister, Laura. She had a great big grin on her face, and a cool fall breeze tousled her hair as she stood there in a pair of jeans and an old Animaniacs T-shirt.

Thoroughly amused, she waited for Will to catch his breath, then pointed to a spot on the ground in front of her. "Let's go again."

Rubbing his shoulder, Will went to the spot and turned to face her.

"Now," Laura said, dropping into a combat stance, "you have to protect your center of mass. Plant your feet."

Will shifted his feet, mirroring the way Laura was standing.

"Good. You ready?"

Will nodded.

Laura instantly closed on him, grabbing his right arm and locking it in a grip. "Okay, I've already got your arm. Not a good start. What do you do? Do you take it back?"

"No," Will said, thinking. "I let you keep it."

"Okay, then what?"

"If I let you keep my arm, I can go for *your* center of mass." Will stepped into Laura's hold, then pushed against her at an angle, knocking her off balance.

Laura fell back, releasing him. "Good, that's good." Without missing a beat, Laura caught herself and sprang quickly back to her feet. "Now what do you—"

CRACK! Will planted a jab right into Laura's chin.

Will stopped, horrified. "Oh god, Laura, I'm sorry, I didn't think—"

She laughed, wiping a small trickle of blood from her chin. "There he is. Knew some of my lessons had to have stuck. C'mon, Rocky, let's see what you've got."

"Wait, what?"

"You heard me, put 'em up."

"Are you kidding? I'm not going to fight you."

"Why?" Laura said, grinning again. "Afraid to fight a girl?"

"Yes! Cause you'll kick my ass."

"Only one way to find out."

Laura immediately went on the attack. Will tried to defend himself, but Laura came from every direction at once. Punches, leg sweeps, spinning kicks—it was like trying to fight a tornado. Will got out a few punches of his own, but they either only found air or were deflected as Laura danced around him.

As Will ducked away from another assault, he finally drove a punch into Laura's gut and connected. Hard.

Laura stumbled back a step, locking Will's arm against her stomach.

She smiled. "Looks like I win."

Realizing he was trapped now, Will desperately tried to pull his arm back—

But it was too late. Laura threw him over her shoulder and back into the dirt.

"That's enough for today," Laura called behind her as she walked back to the house.

"Okay. Sounds good," Will replied, his face in the dirt and his ass in the air.

───────

Once Will pulled himself out of the dirt, he hobbled through the house and out onto the front porch, where he sank into a waiting Adirondack chair.

It wasn't long before Laura came out with a pair of ice-cold beers. She offered him one, which Will gratefully took. After a long sip, he pressed the beer into his face like a cold compress. "Oh, that's the stuff."

Laura snickered, dropping into the Adirondack next to him. "You okay over there?"

Will responded from under the beer. "What are you talking about? I fought a Navy SEAL and lived. This is what victory looks like." Will moved the beer to another sore spot on his arm. "Though if you have six more of these, I wouldn't say no."

They both laughed, then sat and drank in silence for a while.

"What's wrong?" Will asked after a bit.

"Hmmm?"

"Something's wrong. There's a weird quiet you get when something's wrong. What is it?"

Laura smiled, but it was tinged with sadness. "We're going through some... changes at work. I'm not sure how I feel about it yet."

"What kind of changes?"

Laura was quiet for a moment, playing with the black bead bracelet around her wrist. "I'm joining a different group. The work is potentially a lot more dangerous, and it'd mean I'd see you and Dad less."

"Is that why you've been pushing the friendly sparring lessons again?"

"Yeah. I'm not going to be around as much, so I want to make sure you can take care of yourself."

Will laughed. "What, you think someone's going to come attack us?"

He waited for a grin or laugh to show his sister was kidding, but it didn't come. He had never seen her conflicted like this before. Whatever was going on, it had her really worried.

"Are you excited about the new group?" he asked.

"Yeah," Laura said, "I really am."

"Then do it. Dad and I'll be fine." He clinked his beer bottle into hers. "Go out there and save the world."

Laura smiled. "Deal."

"Now if you don't mind, I need to heal." Will settled back into his chair, put his beer back on the right side of his face, and closed his eyes.

As the dream faded, Will woke up to a long, sustained rumbling sound. Opening his eyes, he found himself inside the fuselage of a giant plane.

He wasn't alone, either. Seats lined either side of the fuselage, filled with passengers in varying states of confusion or consciousness. One was a big bald guy, who kinda looked like Mr. Clean. Another was a short, pudgy little man who was quietly muttering to himself. Will heard crying coming from somewhere, but he couldn't tell where.

Across the aisle from him sat a woman with a convention name tag that read "Hello, my name is ANNA." She was frightened but tried to smile at Will.

He smiled back. "I take it this isn't your regular flight either?"

Anna shook her head, her eyes still wide. "No..."

"Hey Anna, my name's Will. Let's you and I make a

deal. Whatever this is, we're in it together now. I'll look out for you, and you look out for me, okay?"

"Quit yapping!" yelled a guard as he walked between them. Will put his head down as the guard passed, then looked back up at Anna and nodded. She gratefully nodded back.

Turning to watch the guard move down the aisle, Will saw there were two guards patrolling back and forth as they watched the passengers. The pudgy little man in a seat further down kept trying to get their attention, but the guards just ignored him.

Will tried to lean forward to whisper to Anna, but his arms didn't come with him. He looked down and saw wide metallic restraints around his wrists. He pulled at them, but they wouldn't budge.

"Don't bother. That's inch-thick steel. We're trussed up nice an' tight."

Will looked to his right, and saw the voice belonged to a big farm boy in a Gettin' Lucky in Kentucky T-shirt. He looked like he was around Will's age, somewhere in his mid-twenties.

"Name's Travis," he said, careful to keep his voice low. "I'd shake your hand, but—" Travis nodded to his own shackled hands.

Will continued to look around the plane. "How long have we been flying?"

Travis shrugged. "Not sure. I've been up for a bit, and we were already flying when I woke up."

Will gave a nod, only half listening. He could see through the window behind another passenger's head that it was still dark outside. Was it still the same night? How long had he been out?

Through the window, he saw nothing under the moon but endless water to the horizon. They were over the ocean. That meant they'd already left the country. Soon, they could be anywhere.

He was about to disappear, just like his sister.

Panic rose at the back of his throat, but he forced himself to stop. What had Laura always said? *If you want to stay alive, first you have to stay calm.* Will took a deep breath and tried to steady his nerves.

"Hey, you okay?" Travis prodded, sounding concerned.

"Just give me a minute."

Will started again, focusing on his surroundings. He was in a plane, which looked like a military model from what little he could see. He tried to remember every plane he'd worked on when he was in air force technical training. Was it a C-130? He'd have to see more of it to be sure.

He also needed a plan. If he figured out what type of plane this was, maybe he could cause an emergency and force it to turn back. All he had to do was get into the electrical system, then he could break all kinds of things.

Will started feeling better. This was an engineering problem. He could do this.

But first he had to get out of his seat.

Will called out to the guards. "Hey, I need to go to the bathroom."

One of the guards waved him away. "Hold it."

Will squirmed in his seat. "I can't. I need to go."

"And I said hold it."

The other guard watched Will wriggling in his seat, then turned to the first guard. "You really want him to piss all over the floor?"

The first guard snarled under his breath, then went to a control panel on the wall. He pressed a button, and Will's restraints sprang open.

The guard prodded Will through a door and into the crew quarters, where Carter was talking to another Fractal agent. Carter noticed Will but quickly looked away. Will tried to say something, but the guard shoved him onward.

They went through another door into a communications room. A large monitor on the wall was tracking the plane's path over the Pacific Ocean, showing them already far past the western coast of the United States. There were multiple computer consoles integrated into the walls, and next to them another Fractal agent was at a terminal, talking to someone through a headset. To his left was a panel with the unmistakable circular ports of a mission computer. Will made a note of that as he kept walking.

The next section was very cramped, with a door on either side of the walkway. The guard stopped and pointed at one. Will opened it to find a small bathroom on the other side.

The guard pushed Will from behind. "Make it fast."

Closing the door behind him, Will looked around the small bathroom. He was sure this was a C-130 now, though he was surprised it had a full bathroom. He'd been expecting a fold-down toilet near the cargo ramp. This plane had been heavily modified from the normal version.

Looking around the tiny room, Will searched for anything he could use to fight back against the guard. The only things he saw were a toilet, a small sink, a paper towel dispenser, and a ceiling light. Nothing that would help in a fight.

Actually, he'd probably lose in a straight fight against the guard anyway. Was there a way to take out the guard without directly fighting him?

Will looked at the light above him again, and gears started turning in his mind. He quickly got to work.

Before long, water was overflowing from the sink, which was now crammed full of paper towels. Water seeped under the door as the guard beat on it from outside. "What's going on in there? Open this door!"

The doorknob rattled as the guard tried to come in. Then a swift kick made the cheap door buckle, and the guard crashed into the bathroom.

He looked up to see Will waiting for him, standing on the toilet in the dark, holding a long cable that ran up into the open light fixture. Before the guard could react, Will dropped the cable into the water.

The cable sparked as the guard jerked and thrashed, then collapsed to the floor.

Once the guard stopped moving, Will reached out and grabbed the cable using a rubber flush valve he'd pried out of the toilet tank. He gave it a quick yank and ripped it out of the light fixture, then threw the now inert cable in the toilet.

Carefully, he tested the water on the ground with the back of his hand. No electric shock.

Will scrambled down off the toilet and pulled the guard further into the bathroom.

After propping the bathroom door up as best he could, Will snuck back into the communications room. The Fractal agent at the terminal had his headphones on, still talking to someone over the radio. It looked like no one had heard him electrocute the guard.

Will let himself exhale. A full five minutes and he wasn't dead yet. Not bad.

Getting back on track, Will went to the next step of his plan. If he was going to sabotage the plane, he'd need a DTADS laptop and interface unit. The mission computer to connect it to was over by the Fractal agent's terminal, but he didn't see the DTADS gear anywhere. It was standard equipment on a plane this size; it had to be somewhere.

Carefully cracking the door open, Will looked into the crew quarters. Carter was still talking to the Fractal agent, but they had their backs to the door. Will took a chance and pushed it open a little further so he could look around the room. There was a rack of weapons on the far wall, some crew gear strewn about, and a stack of charts on the table that Carter and the other man were going through.

But under the table were more boxes of gear, and near the bottom was a black Pelican case.

With DTADS stenciled on the side.

Looking at the case, Will weighed his options. He could go in and try to sneak the case out, but Carter or the Fractal agent would probably hear him. He could also try to wait until they left, but every second he was out here increased his chances of getting caught and locked back in his chair.

Neither were great. As Will debated what he should do, Carter stepped back from the chart. "Honestly, I'm not sure," Carter said. "I'll go ask up front."

The Fractal agent put down his drink. "Fine, I need to hit the head anyway."

Will scrambled back and pressed himself as far as he could into the communication room's wall. Holding his breath, he waited. The Fractal agent walked through the communications room and toward the bathrooms. Will watched to see which way he'd go. *This might be it*, he thought. They'd find the dead guard, and then he'd be caught.

Mercifully, the Fractal agent went into the bathroom without a body in it.

Will immediately dropped down and crept into the

crew quarters. He rifled through the stack of gear under the table, pulled the DTADS Pelican case free, and dragged it back into the communications room.

Now to plug it in. Will looked at the mission computer, which was where he needed to connect the DTADS. It was maybe three feet away from the Fractal agent at the communications terminal. There was no way he'd be able to plug it in without being seen. He'd have to take out the comms agent as well.

Shaking a little, Will pulled a computer out of one of the machine racks. He snuck up behind the comms agent, then smashed the computer into his head.

"Ow, what the f—"

Will panicked as the comms agent turned around, and smashed him in the head again. This time, the agent fell limp in his chair.

Jacked on adrenaline now, Will grabbed the DTADS case and flung it open. He connected the laptop to the interface unit, then patched the whole thing into the mission computer. He turned the laptop on, and after a few seconds, the screen came to life.

DATA TRANSFER AND DIAGNOSTICS SYSTEM
- MAIN MENU -

Will scrolled through menus for electrical systems, flap control, navigation, and other various options until he found the one he wanted—Engines.

Will opened the menu and found the power settings for the plane's engines.

He turned one of them to off.

- ERROR -
AIRCRAFT CURRENTLY REGISTERED AS IN
FLIGHT. ENGINES CANNOT BE POWERED DOWN
FROM THIS CONSOLE.

Shit. Will went back up to the higher menus, looking for settings or config controls. He found an operations profile menu and dug through that. There was a setting for maintenance mode, which he flipped to active. He then switched the plane's status from flying to grounded, which gave him a warning message.

- WARNING -
AIRCRAFT CURRENTLY REGISTERS AS
OPERATIONAL. THIS WILL OVERRIDE TO
GROUNDED STATUS. DO YOU WISH TO
PROCEED?

Will chose to proceed. Now multiple control options lit up as he returned to the main menu. Going back into the engine controls, he had a new option to power cycle the engines. That sounded good. He could power cycle the engines one by one and scare the flight crew into turning back to the US mainland.

Will clicked yes.

A new dialog box popped up.

PERFORMING POWER CYCLING TEST ON ALL
ENGINES, PLEASE WAIT.

All engines? He thought he'd be able to do them one at a time—

Every one of the plane's four engines simultaneously spun down, and shouts came from the front of the plane. Will tried to cancel the engine test, but it was an automated sequence, and he was locked out of the engine controls until the test was done.

He still had access to the other menus. Maybe he could do something else.

The door to the crew quarters flew open, and Carter burst into the communications room. His eyes went from the unconscious Fractal agent on the floor to Will crouched over the DTADS console.

Carter locked the door behind him, then spun back to Will. "What did you do?"

Before Will could answer, the other Fractal agent came back from the bathroom. He lunged at Will, but Carter dove at the Fractal agent and beat him back toward the bathrooms.

Will focused on the DTADS console, looking for anything that could help. He found the control menu for the restraints in the main cabin and set them all to unlock. Numerous shouts came from the front of the plane as captives were set free.

Carter yelled at Will as he fought the Fractal agent. "Whatever you did to the engines, fix it before we all die!"

Will kept digging through menus. "You think I'm going to trust you again?"

Carter's response was cut off as the Fractal agent started strangling him. Will dug down into flap control and found settings for the elevator flaps on the tail. He slightly pitched them down.

The plane lurched under everyone as it tilted toward the ground. Carter and the Fractal agent slid across the floor, drifting past Will and smashing into a computer bank. Carter forced himself free, then broke the Fractal agent's neck.

"Will, fix the plane. Right now."

"Even if I wanted to, I don't think I could," Will said, confused. Carter had tricked him onto this plane, but now he'd just killed a Fractal agent who was about to attack him.

What was going on?

Carter looked out the window. "Never mind, we're too low already." He ran back to unlock the crew quarters door, then grabbed Will's arm. "Time to move."

Carter and Will rushed through the communications room, past the bathrooms, and into the cargo bay at the rear of the plane. Here there were racks and racks of gear and other supplies. Carter pulled down yellow life raft packs as he shoved Will into a jump seat. "Strap in!"

Will fumbled with the seat straps as Carter pulled the inflate tabs on a few of the rafts. Finally, Carter pulled the cargo door release handle, and the back of the plane yawned open.

The water line was rapidly approaching.

Carter dove for the jump seat next to Will, still clutching an uninflated raft. He strapped himself in and pulled the tab on the yellow cube. The raft sprung up around them like a big rubber shield.

Then the plane slammed into the water.

7

DANGEROUS WATERS

SOMEWHERE IN THE PACIFIC OCEAN

THE PLANE HIT the water so hard that it knocked the breath out of Will.

He couldn't see anything from under the yellow raft, but he could feel the plane grinding across the surface of the water. The fuselage groaned and screamed until finally the aircraft came to a stop. Then it rocked backward, and a wave of water smashed into the yellow rubber shield around him.

Carter threw the raft down and undid the restraints on his seat, yelling at Will to do the same. Most of the supplies had come loose from the racks, and water was filling the cargo bay. Through the cargo door was nothing but rolling water and darkness.

"Will!" Carter shouted. "Help me, damnit!"

Will snapped out of it, seeing Carter throwing supplies into one of the rafts. Will helped fill the raft up, then Carter pushed it out the back of the plane.

Water was already up to Will's shins as Carter

pressed an emergency flashlight into his hands. "Hold on to this," he said. Then Carter grabbed Will and threw him into the raft.

A tangle of people clawed into the cargo bay as Will drifted away on the water. Carter helped them into rafts as they came out in groups of three and four. Will recognized Travis and some of the other captives from earlier.

Then there was a horrible, metallic scream, and the front of the fuselage tore off. It dropped away into the ocean as the rest of the plane tilted, sending the tail high up into the air. Screams came from the cargo bay as Carter and the others still inside it disappeared from view.

As the tail tipped up, Will watched in horror as one of the engines started to spin up again. The engine maintenance diagnostic was still running! As the engine spun faster, it sank into the water. Soon it started emitting a piercing whine—

Then it lit up the night as it exploded.

Will curled up in the bottom of his raft as shrapnel flew in every direction. As he poked his head back up, he saw two of the rafts had been flipped in the blast, and some people had been hit with remains of the engine. The explosion had also ignited a patch of fuel on the water, which was now casting an eerie orange glow on the rafts and the remains of the plane.

With a final groan, the tail of the plane disappeared into the water as Will watched it for more survivors. A few more stragglers scrambled out of the cargo bay as the tail submerged, but none of them were Carter.

Then something bumped Will's raft.

He spun around and shined a light on the water behind him. It was the body of the Fractal agent Will had electrocuted in the bathroom. The body was bleeding badly.

Looking around, Will noticed there were a few bodies floating in the water now.

"Shark!" someone screamed to Will's right.

As Will turned franticly, the beam from his light caught a vertical fin right before it disappeared under the surface. Screams broke out in the dark as people in the water desperately paddled for the few remaining rafts.

"Help!" someone screamed to his left.

Will followed the voice and saw Anna swimming as fast as she could. Will crouched on the edge of his raft and paddled toward her. She wasn't far, maybe fifteen feet away. Will paddled harder.

Ten feet.

Five feet.

Anna reached out for the raft but then jerked suddenly. She screamed. Will threw a rope out to her, but Anna jerked again and was pulled under the water.

She didn't come back up.

Over by the oil fire, a new raft shot up out of the water from where the tail of the plane had disappeared. Hanging off a rope tied to it, Carter coughed and spat and cursed as he broke the surface.

Suddenly, the side of Will's raft dropped dramatically as another survivor tried to climb in. "Let me on! Let me on!" the man shouted in a panic.

As the survivor scrambled to climb in, some of the supplies began falling out of the raft. Will grabbed him, trying to help him up. "Hold still, you're going to sink us!"

The man was halfway in when a shark rammed the raft behind Will. The raft flipped, throwing Will, the survivor, and all of the supplies into the ocean. Will's flashlight sank into the depths, rotating end over end. As it spun, its beam briefly revealed multiple sharks circling deep in the water below.

"WILL!"

Whipping his head around, Will followed the shout and saw Travis, motioning him to swim toward him. He had a line ready to throw.

Will swam faster than he'd ever swam before, adrenaline rocketing through his veins. Somewhere behind him he heard the survivor he'd tried to help scream, then trail off into gurgles.

Will kept swimming toward Travis's raft.

Then something punched him hard in the side, and Will saw a dorsal fin retreating off to his right. It took Will a second to realize it wasn't a punch.

A shark had rammed him.

He started swimming again, but now he was turned around and couldn't find Travis's raft. Gunfire rang out, peppering the water around him. Will just kept swimming, trying not to wonder why the shark hadn't eaten him yet. If he just kept swimming, maybe he could get away...

Then an arm wrapped around Will's waist. Carter was in the water with him, turning him. They swam through the water as people screamed and yelled. Soon, they were at a raft, then Carter was lifting Will up into it.

As Carter tried to pull himself up, a shark knocked him away. Will watched numbly as the dorsal fin retreated, then circled around toward Carter again.

Carter saw it and swam to a nearby body in the water. As the shark came for him, Carter shoved the dead body into its open jaws. The shark and the body both disappeared beneath the surface.

An exhausted Carter clambered up into the raft, and quietly lay on his back next to Will. Calls between rafts confirmed that anyone who was still alive was out of the water.

After a while, the rafts all grew quiet, and the only sounds were the waves and the sharks feeding.

8

WITNESS TO TRAGEDY

DIVISION SIX OFFICES - LANGLEY, VIRGINIA

JUST AFTER FOUR in the morning, Maia held an update briefing on the search for Carter Callahan. Bennett and the other senior Division members sat bleary-eyed in the conference room as Maia recounted Carter's path to the Port of Baltimore, and his mysterious disappearance there.

While they asked questions about how Carter got to the port, Maia's phone continued to buzz next to Edgar. After the third time, Edgar picked it up and looked at the screen. He mouthed "Bash" to Maia.

When Bennett asked where Carter was now, Maia was honest: they had no idea. All they could tell was that it looked like he had left the DC area, but they would continue to search just to be sure.

As the briefing group broke up, Maia grabbed her phone and went to the hall to call Sebastian.

He picked up on the first ring. "What took you so long?"

"I have a manhunt to run, remember? I can't take a phone call in the middle of a briefing. What is it?"

"I have a lead. When can I see you?"

Maia lowered her voice and turned down a side hallway. "You shouldn't come back in here, Bash. Bennett will get suspicious if he sees us together again."

"I agree. That is why I am patiently waiting for you in the parking structure."

Maia sighed. "Stay there. I'll be out in five."

Five minutes later, Maia found Sebastian in the parking structure, waiting by her bright red Dodge Charger. "I can't stay long. What have you got?"

Sebastian laid out a few pieces of paper on the hood of her car. "We've been going through the embassy personnel list as we identify who was killed in the blast. So far, one member of the residence staff is still unaccounted for. A clerk that helps with the ambassador's schedule."

Sebastian pointed to the only name on the list that wasn't scratched out: Henry Saunders.

"When you say unaccounted for..."

Sebastian put away the papers. "His body isn't among the dead. From the security footage we have on the network, we know he showed up for his shift at six in the morning, but there's no footage of him leaving. Once the security system came back online after the attack, he was already gone."

"So he left during the security blackout," Maia said, thinking. "Only two reasons to do that. Either he saw something and ran..."

"Or he was in on it," Sebastian finished. "Either way, he won't be in town much longer."

Maia tilted her head. "What are you suggesting?"

"I'm a British national. I can't just go around knocking on doors and forcing my way into someone's apartment. At least, not by myself anyway."

"Bash, CIA officers aren't supposed to do that either. I think you have us confused with the FBI."

Sebastian smiled. "Would you rather I take this to them?"

Maia opened the driver's side door. "Oh get in the damn car."

It was almost five a.m. by the time Maia and Bash pulled up to the Pearl 7 Apartments out by Fort Mahan park. The streets were empty as Maia circled around the building and parked in the back.

She killed her headlights, then turned off the ignition. "You said your clerk is up on the third floor, right?"

Sebastian didn't respond. He was staring at a black sedan parked in the loading zone.

"Bash?"

Sebastian nodded at the sedan. Maia looked at the car and saw three people inside who didn't belong together. The brunette woman behind the wheel looked like a librarian, conservatively dressed, with thin pink glasses. Next to her was a man with thick dreadlocks in a leather jacket. He looked like a lead singer who had lost the rest of his band. In the back seat was a huge guy in a skin-tight T-shirt who had to be some kind of gym rat.

"What do you think those three are doing together out here at five in the morning?" Sebastian said, still watching the sedan.

"Hopefully not asking the same question about us. Let's not wait around to find out."

Maia and Sebastian got out of the car and headed for the building. As they did, Maia pulled a compact out of her purse, pretending to check her makeup. In the compact's mirror, she saw all three heads inside the car turn, following her and Sebastian's every step.

Maia put away the compact and nestled into Sebastian's side. "Put your arm around me."

"What?"

"They're watching us. Put your arm around me."

Sebastian slid his arm around Maia, and they went inside.

As they waited for the elevator, Maia studied the map of the building on the wall. The apartment complex was shaped like a big, boxy figure eight that looped around two courtyards.

Sebastian checked his gun. "Maiara, are you

armed?"

Maia nodded as they watched the hallway that led out to the loading zone, waiting for someone from the sedan to show up.

Thankfully, it stayed empty.

After a few moments, the elevator arrived, and they took it up to the third floor. It was eerily silent as they walked the halls past rows of numbered doors. After a while, they reached the apartment Sebastian was looking for.

He put his ear up to the door, listening. "Someone's inside."

Sebastian looked back at Maia. She answered by drawing her gun and taking position to the left of the doorway.

He nodded, drew his weapon, then knocked on the door. "Mr. Saunders?"

No response.

Sebastian knocked again. "Mr. Saunders, we'd like to speak with you for a moment."

Still no response. Sebastian signaled Maia, who raised her gun.

Then Sebastian kicked in the front door.

It splintered into a trendy living room that was currently unoccupied. A small suitcase lay open on the couch, hastily packed with clothing and a few other items. As Sebastian cautiously went inside, Maia moved to the doorway, her weapon ready.

A streak with purple hair flew past Maia as a man jumped out of the kitchen, catching Sebastian by surprise. The attacker got an arm around Sebastian's neck, but Sebastian flipped him over his shoulder and slammed him into the wood laminate flooring.

Dazed, the man looked up to find two guns pointing back at him.

Now that he was pinned on the floor, Maia got a better look at him. The man had a crooked nose and wild, bright purple streaks in his hair. Multiple piercings in his ear formed a little line of rings that went all the way up from his earlobe to the top.

But the thing Maia noticed most of all was the fear in his eyes. The man was terrified.

Slightly whimpering, the man closed his eyes, bracing himself. "Please, just make it quick."

Maia and Sebastian shared a look, then Maia lowered her gun a bit. "Henry Saunders?"

The man reopened one eye, confused and wary. "Yes?"

Sebastian dropped his gun a bit as well. "We need to talk to you."

It took Henry a moment to make a sentence. "You actually want to talk?"

Sebastian helped Henry up to his feet. "Is anyone else in the apartment?"

Henry shook his head.

"Then you won't mind if I take a look around," Sebastian said, depositing Henry on the couch.

Maia closed the front door, then joined Henry in the living room while Sebastian searched the bedroom.

Henry went first. "Who are you?"

Maia leaned forward. "I'm Maia Calderon. I work for the US government." She gestured at Sebastian as he emerged from the bedroom. "That's Sebastian George, with British Intelligence."

The color drained from Henry's face. "I've heard of Mr. George."

"Then you also know why we're here," said Sebastian, now checking the kitchen. "I have a bunch of dead squaddies at the ambassador's house, and I want to know why you aren't one of them."

Henry's face crumbled. "You have to believe me, I had no idea any of that was going to happen. It was just supposed to be a meeting."

Sebastian ignored him, staring out the window into the courtyard. "Yet here you are, packing. Looks like you're trying to run, Henry."

Henry started to tremble. "You don't understand. These people. I don't have a choice, Mr. George. I have to leave." Shaking, Henry went back to his suitcase, shoving things inside it.

Maia quietly moved to the couch and took a seat next to Henry. "We need to know what happened." She gently took Henry's hand from the suitcase and held it. "I can see that you're scared, which tells me that if you were involved in the attack today, it probably wasn't by choice. Please, help us stop who did this."

Henry sat next to Maia, his shakes subsiding. "I can talk a little, but then I have to go."

"Okay," Maia continued, "let's start with who you're so afraid of."

"About a week ago, a man approached me, asking for a meeting with the ambassador. He said he was some sort of business owner and wanted to talk to the ambassador about a trade agreement. I turned him down, but he was persistent, said he'd make it worth my while. The money he threw at me, I didn't know how to say no."

That got Sebastian to turn from the window. "Was it worth what happened this morning?"

"Of course not!" yelled Henry, horrified. "I thought he just wanted a meeting. I really needed the money, but if I had known—"

"What did you need the money for?" Maia asked as Sebastian turned back to the window.

"My dad. He's sick, and the hospital bills just keep coming," Henry said, unraveling. "I'm already underwater, and this was enough money to wipe out all his bills, and then some."

Sebastian tensed at the window, just for a moment.

But Maia saw it. "What is it?"

"Not sure," Sebastian replied, staring outside. "Thought I saw something on the roof."

"What did he ask you to do?" Maia gently prodded, turning back to Henry.

"All he wanted was for me to get him on the ambassador's meeting list. He was very particular, it had to be on a Sunday, and early."

"Lowest staff presence, skeleton defense crew. Perfect time to attack," Sebastian spat from the window.

Henry hung his head. "I didn't think about that."

"You got him a meeting, then what happened?" Maia

asked.

"He came this morning and had another fellow with him. Tall guy with a briefcase."

"Wait," Maia interrupted, "there were two men?"

"Yes, the man I originally talked to and the one with the briefcase."

Maia had been right. Randall Emerson hadn't acted alone. "So they came to see the ambassador, then what happened?"

"The one with the briefcase went into the ambassador's study, but the other man didn't follow. He turned around and left through the front door."

"He left the building? You're sure?"

Henry nodded. "He left right after the other one went into the study."

"What happened then?" Maia pressed.

"I don't know," said Henry. "I went on break right after that and was eating my snack in the park across the street when... when it happened."

Maia started to ask another question when Sebastian hissed for both of them to be quiet.

"Bash, what are you—" Maia started as she looked up at Sebastian and the window, just in time to see a small glint of moonlight reflected from the adjacent rooftop.

"GUN!" Sebastian shouted, diving over the couch and taking Henry and Maia with him. A half second later, the window shattered, and the spot on the couch where Henry had sat exploded in a burst of upholstery.

Maia wriggled free from Sebastian and crawled

toward the kitchen.

"Maiara, what are you doing?"

Ignoring him, Maia jumped up and ran to the far wall. As soon as she reached it, she slapped the switch for the living room lights.

The room went pitch black, except for a small patch of moonlight by the window.

"I can't see!" screamed Henry.

"Neither can they," Maia bit out in a whisper. "Keep your voice down. Your eyes will adjust in a minute."

As they waited, a red laser appeared through the window and began floating around the room.

"We're going to die, we're going to die," muttered Henry, terrified.

Maia watched the laser drift toward her. "Bash?"

"Yes?" came Sebastian's voice from somewhere near the window.

"Curtain."

As the laser swept by, Maia crept along in the darkness to the left side of the living room window. By the time she reached it, she could make out Sebastian standing on the right side, pressed against the wall.

They nodded to each other, then whipped the curtain closed.

Maia and Sebastian rolled away from the window just as Henry flung open the front door and fled into the hallway.

"I've got him," Maia shouted, bolting for the door.

"I'll take sniper," replied Sebastian, hot on her heels.

When they reached the hallway, Maia raced after

Henry, and Sebastian split off toward a stairway marked Roof Access.

Maia caught up with Henry at the bank of elevators just as the left elevator opened. Inside it was The Librarian from the black sedan, already reaching for her gun.

Henry pivoted toward the stairwell as The Librarian turned her weapon toward Maia.

Maia was faster and shot the woman twice in the shoulder. She howled in pain and fell back into the elevator.

More gunshots rang out from somewhere above her. Hoping Sebastian was okay, Maia plowed into the stairwell, where she heard Henry cry out in pain from the floor below. Maia flew down the stairs until she found Dreadlocks strangling Henry on one of the landings. Maia hurled herself at the man, sending both of them tumbling down another set of stairs in a knot of angry limbs. Slamming into the next landing, they cracked apart.

Dizzy from the fall, Maia wobbled to her feet as Dreadlocks attacked again. A punch hit Maia in the head, and her vision swam. She socked Dreadlocks in the stomach and knocked the wind out of him. A well-placed kick sent him reeling away from her, then a second one sent him over the railing. Maia heard him land with a sickening crunch at the bottom of the stairwell.

Stumbling back up the stairs, Maia grabbed Henry, then headed down. As they reached the door to the first floor, Maia heard a noise behind them.

Looking down, she saw Dreadlocks. He was still alive, but his back was broken. In spite of that, he was slowly crawling across the floor, his blank eyes staring right at Maia.

Who *were* these people?

Forcing her fear down, Maia pushed Henry through the door, and they ran for the lobby—

Where they found Gym Rat waiting in front of the main doors. Surprised to see them, Gym Rat wasn't able to pull his gun before Maia fired at him, forcing him to hide behind the lobby sofa set.

Maia grabbed Henry and pulled him back around the corner and down the hall. Endless apartment doors lined either wall.

"Henry, where's another exit?" she asked.

Terrified, Henry muttered incoherently.

She knew they only had seconds before Gym Rat would come around the corner. "We'll have to make our own then."

Maia turned to the nearest door and fired twice around the lock, then kicked the door open. She pulled Henry in after her, slamming the door shut behind them. Through the living room windows, Maia could see the courtyard was only a few feet below. She tried to open the window but couldn't find a latch or a handle to slide it with.

It was a fixed window, the kind that wasn't built to open.

"We're trapped!" Henry yelled. "There's no way out of here!"

"Will be in a second," Maia said, picking up a chair. She hurled it through the window, opening a way out to the courtyard. She knocked away the remaining broken glass with the barrel of her gun.

"Move it, Henry!" Maia said, pushing him through the open window. Henry cried out in surprise as he fell down to the courtyard.

Before Maia could jump, the door flew open and Gym Rat began firing at her. Maia dove out of the way, then fired back, forcing Gym Rat out into the hall. She ran for the window and jumped through it, falling to the courtyard below.

As her feet hit the ground, she grabbed Henry and tore across the garden area. Running as fast as she could, Maia saw the red laser again, swinging in front of them to intercept their path. Maia yanked Henry hard to the right, but the laser swung up and away.

Maia risked a look behind her and saw Sebastian fighting with the sniper on the roof. Gym Rat had also made it to the shattered living room window, aiming his weapon at her. Throwing Henry to the ground, Maia dove again as Gym Rat fired. Never stopping, she rolled, popped up in a crouch, and fired back.

Gym Rat's head jerked, and he fell backward into the shadows of the apartment.

Lights blinked on in windows around the complex

as residents started waking up from all the noise. The place would be crawling with police soon, Maia thought.

They needed to get out of here.

Maia grabbed Henry and ran for the courtyard exit. As they reached it, she shoved Henry inside, then looked back at the roof. Sebastian collapsed as the sniper kicked him in the head. Maia yelled and fired at the sniper, then ran inside after Henry.

Once they finally reached the parking lot, Maia dragged Henry to her car and told him to get inside. Running for the driver's side door, Maia stopped when she saw her tires. They were flat. Someone had slashed them.

Her car wasn't going anywhere.

Henry came over to see what she was looking at, and his eyes went wide when he saw the tires. "Oh no, what do we do now?"

As Maia thought about where to go next, an engine revved off to her left, and headlights flared on—

It was the black sedan from the loading zone, headed right at her and Henry.

Maia shoved Henry behind her car for protection just as the sedan slammed into her. Instinct took over, and she did her best to shoulder roll up onto the hood of the car. Maia covered her head with her arms as she smashed into the windshield, cracking the glass as she collided.

Clinging to the hood of the sedan for dear life, Maia held on as the sedan swerved back and forth, trying to throw her off. Through the cracked glass, Maia saw The Librarian from the elevator in the driver's seat. Her right arm was still limp from where Maia had shot her in the shoulder.

Maia pulled her gun and fired.

Click. It was empty.

The Librarian grinned and poured on the gas, heading straight for the building at the end of the parking lot.

Maia used her gun as a hammer, repeatedly smashing it into the windshield. The cracked glass quickly gave way, and soon Maia had made a hole big enough to fit through. She crawled into the passenger seat and put on the seatbelt.

Realizing what Maia was doing, The Librarian reached over to strangle Maia with her good arm.

Instead of fighting back, Maia reached down and released The Librarian's seatbelt.

The car slammed into the wall, and The Librarian shot through the windshield like a water balloon fired from a slingshot. She sailed through the air and smashed into the wall of the parking garage next door.

Maia repeatedly kicked the passenger side door until it lurched open, then stumbled out of the car. She looked at what was left of The Librarian plastered across the parking garage wall, then turned back to the apartment complex's parking lot. "Henry?"

Henry's head popped up like a gopher from between two cars. "You're still alive?"

"I'm as surprised as you are. Come on."

Maia and Henry stumbled out onto Minnesota Avenue, but they were running on fumes. They forced their way across a strip mall parking lot and toward another set of buildings across the street. *If we could just get far enough away,* Maia thought, *I could hide Henry and call for help.*

Then the red laser appeared between Henry's shoulder blades.

Maia jerked him to the side just as a shot rang out behind them. A sniper bullet knocked a crater in the sidewalk.

Out of options, Maia put Henry behind her and turned to face the sniper. She pulled out her CIA badge and held it up.

"I'm sure you have a scope on that thing," Maia shouted, waving her badge. "Can you read this?"

She looked down and saw the red laser hovering over her heart.

Henry was shaking behind her. "Please. Please, I don't want to die. I'm sorry."

"If you shoot me, you'll be killing a federal officer," Maia shouted at the silhouette standing on top of the apartment complex. "So if you want to kill this man, you're going to have to kill me to do it."

The laser continued wandering around Maia's upper

torso, but no bullet came.

After what felt like an eternity, the red dot swung away and swept up a nearby utility pole. A shot rang out, and the transformer above Maia and Henry exploded. They both ducked, instinctively moving away from the blast.

Then Maia heard a second shot, and Henry dropped to the ground next to her.

He was dead.

She turned back to the roof of the apartment building.

The sniper was gone.

By the time Maia made it to the roof of the apartment building, she could see police cars converging on the parking lot below. She didn't care if she was caught anymore, she just wanted to know if Sebastian was okay.

She found him still crumpled at the spot above the courtyard where the sniper had knocked him down. Maia's heart jumped into her throat. From somewhere deep down, she found a little more juice and ran the rest of the way to where Sebastian was lying.

Maia crouched over him, checking for vitals. She felt a pulse. His breathing was shallow, but she could see his chest rise and fall.

He was alive.

The last of Maia's adrenaline ebbed, and she fell down next to him.

He stirred, then slowly opened his eyes. "So you do care about me."

Maia punched him in the shoulder. "Don't ever scare me like that again."

"The clerk?"

Maia shook her head. "I thought you were dead."

"So did I. She had me cold."

"She?"

Sebastian smiled. "The sniper. I know a woman when I see one. Highly skilled. Shot the gun out of my hand as soon as I got on the roof."

"But she didn't kill you."

Sebastian winced as he sat up. "I suppose not."

"She could have shot me too, but she didn't. I wonder why..."

"Maybe she wasn't allowed to."

Maia looked at Sebastian, confused.

"Whoever she was, she wasn't working alone," Sebastian said. "There was someone talking to her, over a headset."

"Maybe it was one of the crew from the sedan?"

"No," Sebastian said, lying back down. "The way she talked to them, it was a superior. She was taking orders."

"This is a lot of firepower to send after one witness," Maia said, staring at the police cars gathering below. "Whoever these people are, they don't want anyone looking into what happened at the embassy."

"Maiara, what the devil is going on here?"

Maia wasn't sure. But she was determined to find out.

9

RAFT LIFE
SOMEWHERE IN THE PACIFIC OCEAN

THE FIRST THING Will noticed when he woke up was that something wet was covering him. His mouth was dry, and his face was stuck to whatever he was lying on. Still half asleep, it took him a minute to remember what had happened.

Carter. Being kidnapped.

The plane crash.

Oh shit, where am I?

Will peeled his face off the bottom of the raft and sat bolt upright, yanking the damp shroud off of him. He blinked as the sun stung his eyes, then looked down at the wet thing in his hand. It was Carter's jacket.

"Morning, sunshine."

Still groggy, Will saw Carter sitting in the raft next to another man with a gash in his head. He was pale and unconscious, but Will recognized him. He was one of the guards from the plane.

And in the middle of the raft was a shark.

Panicking, Will backed up so fast he almost fell overboard and into the ocean.

"Whoa, whoa. Easy, kid," Carter called after him. "It's dead, look."

Carter poked the shark with a paddle, but it just lay there, motionless. Now that Will was really looking at it, he noticed a chunk had been torn off the side of the shark's body. It looked pretty dead.

Will settled back into the raft, taking a look around. Endless stretches of blue ocean spread out to the horizon in every direction. Scattered across the rolling waves were the remaining survivors, staying afloat on a handful rafts and a few chunks of the plane. The little flotilla had drifted apart during the night, and survivors had to shout to talk to the other rafts.

"They're all pretty far away," Carter said. "They won't be able to hear us."

Will responded by handing Carter his jacket.

Carter held it over the side, ringing the water out. "Didn't want you to burn up in the sun. You can't drink seawater, but you can use it to keep cool so you don't sweat or burn."

Next to the shark, Will saw that Carter had cut off a few chunks of meat. Just looking at them made his stomach growl. He reached for a piece, but Carter slapped his hand away with the oar.

"Don't eat that."

Will finally popped. "What is *wrong* with you? You say you want to help me find my sister, then you get me kidnapped. You save me from dying in the plane, but now you want me to starve to death. While you make up your mind if you want me dead or not, I'm at least going to eat something." Will reached out for a piece of shark.

Carter slapped Will's hand away again, harder this time. "You can't eat that because I'm using it to poison our friend here." He motioned to the unconscious Fractal agent. "Dehydration and heat stroke are a potent combo, and combined with the levels of mercury in that shark meat, I've basically put him in a coma. Honestly, you should be thanking me. Before I put him under, he was talking about eating you."

Will sat back in frustration. After a few moments of silence, he looked back at Carter. "Why me?"

"What?"

"You heard me. Why me? You had this entire plane full of people that you and your friends kidnapped. But you actively sought me out, hunted me down."

"Will—"

"And you dangled my sister in front of me. How could you *do* that? I'd do anything for a chance to see her again, Carter. You used that, perverted it to trick me into whatever the hell this is. If my sister did ever know you, she'd be disgusted by you now. What kind of monster would—"

Carter jabbed the raft oar into Will's throat, cutting him off. "You're done talking now. Sit there and be quiet."

Will didn't say a word, and after a minute Carter pulled the oar away.

"Good," Carter said, setting the oar down. Then he looked out at the water, staring at the horizon. Silent.

"Laura Taylor is one of my best friends," he finally said after awhile. "I was with her when she was stationed in Kandahar, and I should have been with her when she disappeared. The day she went missing, our team was sent to investigate a potential enemy base, but I got reassigned at the last minute to another mission. When I got back, Laura's team hadn't made contact in over three hours.

"Every night since then, I lie awake wondering what would have happened if I'd gone with them," Carter said, softer now. Will could hear the pain in his voice. "Maybe I could have prevented all of this, or maybe I'd just be dead and it would have played out the same."

Carter watched the water rise and fall against the horizon. "When she went missing, I dropped all of my agency assignments and went after her. I must have turned over every rock south of the Arghandab looking for your sister, but she'd vanished, like a ghost. After a few weeks, the agency gave me an ultimatum: return to my sanctioned assignments, or come home to Langley. I chose option three, told the deputy director to jump up his own ass, and went rogue so I could continue looking for Laura."

"So you're not with the CIA anymore?"

"Not the point," Carter said, looking back at Will. "After weeks on my own, I finally found a lead that pointed to Laura being taken by an organization I'd never heard of: Fractal. I found a way to infiltrate one of their teams in Afghanistan, and I've been a mole inside ever since. When I told you I'd tracked your sister from Chicago to Honduras to Malaysia, it was because I was chasing her through Fractal as a low-level agent. I've been inside almost a year now, but that picture of your sister chained up in a truck is proof she's still out there."

Carter cleared his throat. "I wasn't trying to trick you into doing this, but having you come in as a captive was the only way I could get you onto Palmyra without raising suspicion. If I had told you what was going to happen, you would have given yourself away to Specs, and you'd probably be dead by now."

"Carter, I—"

"*Save it*," Carter snarled, dunking his jacket in the water. "I told you this would be dangerous, and now you know it is. I haven't slept in two days, and I'm exhausted. Wake me up if anyone starts dying, and try not to crash the raft while I'm asleep."

Carter pulled his jacket over his head and went to sleep, leaving Will alone with his thoughts.

While Carter slept, Will passed the time watching the other survivors. The people in Travis's raft were sleeping in shifts, with one person always looking out for land. The two survivors on the broken wing of the plane had gotten ahold of one of the damaged rafts and rigged it like a giant tent canopy, protecting them from the sun. One raft had two prisoners that wouldn't stop crying, while another raft was full of Fractal agents bickering over a movie trivia game.

One man was in a raft by himself and hadn't moved in a while. He was still curled up in a ball around a bag he must have saved from the plane. Will wondered what could be in it that would make him cling to it so tightly.

Nearby, Carter rustled under his jacket as Will continued to watch the ocean toss the little group about. "I miss anything?" Carter asked, sitting up.

Will shook his head.

Carter got up on his knees, grabbed the oar, and crawled over to the edge of the raft. The other end of the oar had been sharpened into a spearpoint, which Carter now held as he watched the water.

"Carter?" Will asked quietly.

"What?"

"Did I kill all these people?"

Carter jabbed at the water. "Kid, you crashed an airplane. Depending on how I look at it, that should make me furious or impress the hell out of me."

"Which one did you choose?"

"Haven't decided yet." Carter jabbed at the water again. "But you didn't put any of those people on that plane. Every Fractal you killed is one less we have to deal with."

"What about the prisoners? Anna?"

"Honestly? Fractal would have killed most of them anyway. You just spared them a lot of pain." Carter stabbed the water, and this time came back with a fish on the end of the oar. Grabbing his knife, Carter cleanly sliced it apart, then offered half of it to Will.

"Is it safe to eat raw?"

"Safer than starving to death," Carter said, taking a bite. "Go on, saltwater kills most of the bacteria, and worms in saltwater fish are big enough that you can see them. If you can't see any, you're good."

Will checked the fish for worms, then gratefully tore into it. Within moments, it was gone.

Carter tossed the remains of the fish into the water. "You need to understand that you and I are effectively inside a terrorist organization now. We are going to find Laura, but there's more to it than that. Fractal's ramping up for something big. That attack on the embassy was just the start of it. Most of the Fractal operations I've seen since I've been inside have all been quiet stuff. Hired assassinations, kidnapping, and so on. Whatever this is, it's on a much larger scale. I think this is building to some kind of attack, and I've got to find a way to stop it."

Carter quickly rinsed his knife in the ocean and put it away. "That's why I need you. I can't cover an entire atoll and find Laura before whatever Fractal has planned goes into action. As a trainee, you'll have access to areas of Palmyra I won't. You also know your sister better than anyone on the planet. If there's anyone who can help me find her, it's you."

Will nodded. "We'll find her."

"Damn right we will. We have to be careful though. We can't let anyone find out our real identities. Fractal went through a lot of trouble to get to your sister, so I imagine they'd be pretty interested in you as well. We can't let them know who you really are."

"What about you?"

Carter laughed. "That's easy. They figure out I'm CIA, they'll just have someone kill me. Maybe give me a little torture first, see what I know."

"But you're not CIA anymore, right?"

"Doesn't matter, they'd kill me just to be safe."

Will let that sink in for a minute, thinking.

Carter sat back and kicked his feet up on the edge of the raft. "That's it. That's everything out on the table."

"So let me get this straight. We're going to the secret base of a terrorist organization. On a Pacific island."

"Atoll. It's an atoll."

"Fine. We're going to a secret terrorist base on an atoll, in the Pacific Ocean, to rescue my sister and stop some massive attack they have planned…"

"Glad to see you've been listening."

"You know what this is, right?"

Carter cocked an eyebrow at Will. "The culmination of multiple poor life choices?"

"No," Will said, almost excited. "It's James Bond shit."

"Jesus Christ, kid. If that's your takeaway from all this, we may be more screwed than I thought."

"Look around, Carter. This doesn't look like a diner."

"I'd stab you right now if it meant I could be in a diner instead of out here."

Will and Carter shared a laugh, then fell quiet as

they watched the ocean.

"I gotta ask," Carter said. "Your stunt with the plane, what was your plan exactly? You realized you were *on* the plane you were crashing, right?"

"I wasn't trying to crash it. I was trying to create an emergency so the plane would be forced to turn around and land."

"We were less than an hour out from Palmyra. The closest runway by that point was the one we were going to."

"I didn't know! I was drugged and kidnapped by a group of maniacs." Will leaned back into the raft wall. "Got me off the plane though."

Carter rubbed his eyes. "I'm beginning to see why Billy Dibecki used to torture the shit out of you." After Will's stunned look, Carter continued, "I must have heard that story from Laura a hundred times. She was so proud."

A thready voice came from the back of the raft. "You crashed the plane?"

Carter and Will both turned to see the Fractal agent sitting up, his eyes open. Will wondered how much he had heard.

"Boat!" someone screamed from another raft.

Survivors from multiple rafts all began to shout as they pointed to the west. Sure enough, two little white dots on the horizon were slowly turning into boats.

As the other survivors cheered, the Fractal agent in Will's raft became more and more animated. "You crashed the plane? You tried to kill us all! Help! Help!"

10

WELCOMING COMMITTEE

SOMEWHERE IN THE PACIFIC OCEAN

JUST AS THE Fractal agent tried to get up, Carter punched him in the throat. The Fractal fell back, coughing and sputtering.

Carter quickly pinned him to the bottom of the raft. "Watch the others. See if anyone is looking over here."

Will turned back and saw the boats approaching the first group of survivors. Everyone was so excited to see them that no one was paying attention to what was going on in Will's raft. The boats were coming from the far side, so they would get to their raft last. "They're distracted. It looks like—"

Will's voice broke off as he turned to see Carter with his knife out, still holding down the Fractal agent. Carter's knife disappeared into the base of the Fractal's skull, then the man's eyes unfocused as he twitched once and went still.

Carter quickly flipped the body over to slow the blood from going everywhere. He began coiling the rope from the raft around the body, stopping only to hand Will his knife. "Cut the line free."

Will bent over the rope, stealing glances at the other rafts while he worked. The survivors from Travis's raft were getting pulled onto one of the boats. They were close enough now that Will could see Marine Conservation Society logos on the side of the hull.

It wouldn't be long before they reached their raft.

Will cut through the rope, then tossed the end to Carter, who took it and immediately started coiling it around the dead shark. Then he looped the rope around the dead Fractal, pulling them together.

"Knife," Carter said without looking up.

Will held the knife out to Carter, but he didn't take it.

"No, stab here," Carter said, pointing to a spot on the shark's belly between the two pectoral fins.

"What? Why do—"

"No time, just do it."

Will stabbed where Carter pointed, and a little blood came out.

Carter kept lashing the dead body to the shark. "Keep going. Move down an inch or two each time until it works."

Will wanted to ask until what worked, but thought better of it. He stabbed the shark again. Another small blood trickle. Will moved down some more, then stabbed again. Blood trickle.

He moved the knife down and stabbed again. This time, a torrent of oily, foul-smelling goo came out.

"Good," Carter grunted.

Will checked where the boats were. They were rescuing the last group of rafts before theirs.

"Grab his feet," Carter barked.

They picked up the dead Fractal and rolled him over the side of the raft and into the ocean. Carter quickly grabbed the shark and shoved it overboard as well. The shark sank immediately, disappearing into the dark blue water. After a moment, the rope went taught, and then the dead Fractal was pulled under as well.

Carter tore off his jacket and used it to mop up as much of the blood and shark goo as he could. Will tried to help by scooping some over the side of the raft. "What is this stuff?"

"Shark liver oil. Sharks need their liver to help float. The less oil in their liver, the faster they sink." Carter balled up his jacket and stuffed it under the raft. "Stop cleaning, it's good enough."

Will and Carter sat back in the raft as one of the rescue boats headed their way.

———

It was cramped in the stern of the boat, but Will was just grateful to be out of the water. The rescue boats were some kind of fishing vessels and had definitely not been built to hold this many people. Between survivors and the boat's crew, Will counted at least fifteen people, with about as many packed into the second boat as well.

There was a water jug going around, which the survivors took long, greedy chugs from. As they did, a short crew member with a plastic smile had taken it upon himself to greet them all. He reminded Will of a bad tour guide he'd seen on a vacation once when he was a kid. All teeth and fake smile.

Tour Guide brought over another jug of water for the survivors to drink from. "Here you go. We have more water if you need it."

From the back, one of the survivors piped up. "How'd you find us?"

Tour Guide flashed a big smile. "We have a weather radar system at our research lab. Your plane showed up on it, then suddenly disappeared. We were worried you'd crashed, so we took two of the boats and came out here to see what happened."

"Where are we going?" another voice rang out.

"We have a research station on an island nearby," Tour Guide said. "We'll take you back, get you fed, then figure out how to get you all where you need to go."

Inside the boat's tiny cabin, Will could see the man with the bag from the raft animatedly discussing something with the captain. Even now, he was clutching the bag protectively, shielding it like a newborn. He alternated between talking to the captain and glaring at the passengers in the stern.

Travis nudged Will in the side, passing him the jug of water. Will took it and sucked water out of the jug for almost a solid minute.

"Easy," Travis said, tipping the jug down. "Drink too fast, you'll make yourself sick."

Will nodded, took one more pull from the jug, then passed it on. "Thanks," he said, nodding back at Travis.

"I reckon there'll be all the water you can drink once we get to the research station these guys are from."

"Yeah, you're right."

Travis turned to face Will directly. "Let's do this proper." He extended his hand. "Travis Clarkson."

Will turned to meet him. "Will Kirby." He reached out and shook Travis's hand.

"Pleased to meet you, Will."

"Heh, you too, Travis."

Travis gave Will a pat on the back. "Glad you made it, brother." He leaned back and closed his eyes. "We're safe now."

Despite being out of the water, Will didn't feel safe. While Tour Guide seemed fake but harmless, the other two crew members looked out of place. They were tall, imposing, and surprisingly fit. That research station must have one hell of a CrossFit program.

Will watched as the pudgy little man he'd seen on the plane went up to the two crewmen and offered them the empty water jug. The one on the right took it and headed to the front of the boat.

The pudgy man smiled up at the other crewman and stuck out his hand. "Howard Foster. Pleased to meet ya!"

The crewman didn't shake it.

Howard, however, didn't take the hint. "Always nice to meet a fellow ocean warrior. You guys are pretty far out here. What kind of work are you doing? You studying reef bleaching? Establishing a protected area? Following migration patterns?"

The crewman looked at him blankly. "We study the fish."

"Oh yeah?" Howard replied, just getting warmed up. "Which group are you guys with? Glories? HSA? We probably know some of the same—"

The crewman shoved him away. "You can ask scientists at research station. They know all about the fish."

Before Howard could dig any deeper, the crewman went over to the port rail and began checking lines that were already very secure.

"Land!" came a shout from the other boat.

The stern on Will's boat emptied out as everyone rushed to get a view of the little island's tree line on the horizon. Carter didn't get up, so Will stayed behind as well.

It wasn't long before they were the only two left in the stern. As everyone crowded around the bow of the boat to get a better look, Will silently mouthed to Carter "Are we safe?"

Carter slowly shook his head.

No.

───────

As the fishing boats puttered through the water, the tree line swelled into a full island. Shallow waters lapped at miles of coastline that was made up of sprawling coral reefs. Will watched as all kinds of fish and other sea life darted around the forest of coral, while further out, sharks lazily swam about, waiting for anything adventurous enough to come out into open waters.

The boats swung up and around the coastline until they reached a wide channel that had been cut through the reefs. They turned into it, and sailed through the long trench until it opened up into a beautiful blue lagoon. As the boats moved further in, multiple bits of land were visible sprinkled among the reefs.

"Oh, it's not an island," Howard said from up near the bow, "it's an atoll!"

"That's right," said Tour Guide. "The atoll is made up of a bunch of little islands."

A cold chill shot up Will's spine. An atoll?

He looked at Carter.

Ever so slightly, Carter nodded.

The boats turned and slowly circled starboard, coming to rest at a small dock tucked under a line of trees. Tour Guide turned back to the group. "Here we are. Welcome to Palmyra!"

The survivors piled out of the boats and found a small welcoming committee waiting for them. The captain of Will's boat grabbed the man with the bag and rushed him down the path, disappearing into the trees behind the men waiting along the shore.

"Welcome, welcome," Tour Guide said. "Everyone come forward, gather around!"

The survivors moved forward toward the welcoming group as the two fishing boats pulled away from the dock and headed out into the lagoon.

"Normally we do these kind of things in the hangar when the plane lands," Tour Guide said, "but this will have to do."

Some of the survivors suddenly realized what was going on and became wary. Will noticed the Fractal agents from the plane crash slowly drifting out, forming a circle around them.

Tour Guide gave another big grin. "It's time to begin your orientation. Welcome to Fractal."

Will was shocked at how fast the Fractal agents moved. Between the Fractals from the plane and the welcoming committee, the surviving captives were hopelessly outnumbered. Most of the captives were taken down quickly, but a few fought back. Travis and one of the women were fighting off two Fractals when an arm wrapped around Will's neck and suddenly he was facedown in the dirt.

"Don't move," Carter whispered, pinning him to the ground. He punched Will in the side twice, but pulled his punches enough so that they only stung slightly. "Keep your head down for the rest of this, and you'll be fine."

Carter pulled Will up to his knees just in time for him to see two Fractal agents tackle Travis to the ground.

The Fractals went around binding all of the captives' hands behind their back. As they did, each was pulled back to their feet and pushed into a crude line.

"There we go," said Tour Guide. "Now let's get you to processing."

Soon, the captives were being marched south down the tree-lined path. Between the plane crash, surviving on the rafts, and being beaten by Fractal agents, walking was slow going for most of them. What was left of the captives were in poor shape, and most could barely stay on their feet.

As they continued, the path began to flare out into a small island. The trees were thicker here, and grew together into large knots of tropical foliage overhead. The Fractal agents were leading them toward a low concrete building, carefully hidden amongst the trees. The structure was barely a story tall, and blended in with the surrounding vegetation so well that it would be impossible to see from the water.

Will and the captives were herded inside the building and into a sleek, modern entryway as the Fractals prodded them toward a set of elevators. Once inside, a Fractal agent scanned a key card to make buttons for various floors appear on a touchscreen in the wall. He picked the one titled Processing, and the elevator glided downward.

Moments later, the elevator opened up and deposited them all on the processing floor. The captives were led through a series of stations where they were forced to strip naked, get hosed down, and change into drab gray jumpsuits. Will watched some captives try to fight back as Fractal agents took their personal items, but one by one the captives all relented and fell in line.

At the end of the stations was one final area where a burly Fractal agent slapped a thick black cuff around Will's right ankle. As soon as it closed, a green light on the cuff blinked on.

"What is this?" Will asked, poking at his new accessory.

"GPS tracker, so you don't get lost." The Fractal agent shoved Will forward toward the captives that had already been cuffed.

After another short elevator trip, Will and the other captives were led into a large, octagonal room filled with seats. As the sea of gray jumpsuited captives sat down, the walls above them began to glow.

They weren't walls at all. They were giant monitors.

The lights dimmed as the face of an Argentinian woman in her fifties filled the screens around the room. Her dark hair was pulled back into a bun, and a pair of austere glasses perched on a sharp nose that sat under cold, unblinking eyes. Her face changed as she revealed a broad smile, but Will noticed it didn't reach her eyes. It was an icy grin, the type of expression he had seen predators make on the nature channel.

Right before they ate something.

"Hello, everyone. My name is Dr. Yaras. Welcome to Palmyra."

She dropped her voice a little and began speaking slowly. "You've joined us at an exciting time. Fractal is making great strides to change the world, and each of you will be a part of it in your own way. While you did not choose to come here, I believe some of you will see it as your home, in time."

Dr. Yaras's voice was incredibly melodic and had a deep, hypnotic quality to it. Will imagined it was probably what honey would sound like...

Feeling like he was drifting off to sleep, Will shook himself awake.

Travis looked at Will. "Home?" he said skeptically.

"Now that you have made it to Palmyra," Dr. Yaras continued, "you are officially Fractal trainees. Each of you will undergo a rigorous training program, which will show us where your talents can be of the most use. Once you've completed your assessment, you will work for us and have a chance to earn your freedom."

Around the room, everyone in the chairs was silent, completely transfixed by Dr. Yaras up on the screens. Even Travis was staring at them now, intently focused on what Dr. Yaras was saying. It was like they had all been hypnotized, hanging on her every word.

Looking up above the monitors, Will noticed a small ring of windows further up the wall. Standing at one of them was Dr. Yaras, watching everyone in the chairs below. She caught Will looking at her and tilted her head, studying him for a moment.

The recording continued on the monitors. "Every part mirrors the whole at Fractal. I truly believe that, together, we can accomplish anything. So work hard, prove your worth, and I will set you free." On the screens, Dr. Yaras gave a chilling smile once more. "Now get some rest. We have a great deal of work to do."

Will blinked as the lights came up. While Fractal agents began to get people to their feet and clear the room, Will looked back to the ring of windows above.

Dr. Yaras was gone.

A group of Fractals led Will and the other trainees back to the surface, then marched them east to another camouflaged building. This one was much more sparse than the building they'd just left. It was all exposed concrete with retrofitted tech attached to the walls.

The trainees were led through a guard station inside the entrance, then past a large mess hall. The Fractal agents in front turned left as the corridor wound around the mess hall, then descended a long ramp to the next floor. Here there was what looked like a small hospital, as well as a gym filled with weapons.

The Fractals led them on, following another loop in the corridor and descending down another long ramp to the third floor. This floor was very different than the others. Here there were rows and rows of hallways, each dotted with lines of doors. As the group went, the Fractal agents would occasionally stop at a door and push a trainee inside.

Eventually it was Will's turn, and he soon found himself alone in a cramped concrete room. There was a small bed, a toilet, and a metal sink, but that was it.

"Hello?" he called out.

There was no response.

Will stood silently for a moment, straining to hear anything but the sound of his own breathing. He couldn't hear any of the Fractal agents or trainees in the hall outside. There was nothing but silence. He tried the door, but it didn't budge. There was a card reader on the wall to the left of the door, similar to the one for the elevator. It looked like he needed a key card to activate it.

Will pulled off his shoes and sat on the bed. He'd made it. His sister was somewhere on one of these islands, and he would tear this entire atoll apart if that's what it took to see her again. With Carter's help, he knew they'd find her. He just had to make sure he stayed alive long enough to do it.

Accepting he was stuck in his room for the time being, Will turned his attention to his GPS anklet. It was an older model, but there was a thick protective casing that had been added to it. It was pretty rugged and would do a good job of protecting the anklet against anything on the atoll, including water.

If he was going to sneak around looking for Laura, this anklet was going to have to come off.

Will searched the room for something he could use as a tool. The bed and the toilet yielded no results, but on the sink Will found a small part of the metal exterior that had been bent out from the wall. He pulled on it, and it bent further. Will worked it back and forth until the bit of metal finally gave way and broke free.

He scraped the edge of the metal shard against the concrete for several minutes, then tested it with his finger. It was sharp. Will tried slicing into his anklet with it, and after some work, the metal shard began to cut into the protective outer casing.

Will smiled. It was a start.

Dr. Yaras stood in the middle of a sweeping command center, bristling with monitors and computer terminals. All around the room, Fractal operators hunched over their stations as they spoke to agents scattered around the globe.

Her attention, however, was focused on a large wall screen filled with profiles of her new trainees. The current one was Howard Foster: a marine biologist from New York. As she finished skimming it, Dr. Yaras clicked a small remote, and the screen switched to a new profile. Travis Clarkson's face filled the left side of the screen as she read through his information.

"Doctor?" asked an operator from one of the computers. "There's an incoming call for you."

Dr. Yaras didn't look away from Travis's profile. "Who is it?"

"Scorpion, ma'am. She says you wanted to speak to her."

"Put her up on screen."

Travis's profile disappeared from the monitor, and a live feed of Scorpion took its place.

"Hello, Scorpion. What is your team's status?"

"We're en route to the second target. We should be on site soon. Is the tunnel ready?"

"The drill team is ahead of schedule," Dr. Yaras said. "They will be ready for your arrival."

"I'll check in once we land."

"Before you go, there's an issue we need to discuss."

"Yes?"

Dr. Yaras paused, watching the other woman on the monitor. "The incident at the apartment complex."

"What about it? The target was neutralized."

"Of course it was, I sent you. Losing an entire site team isn't like you, though. That was... unexpected."

"There was unexpected resistance."

"So there was." Dr. Yaras picked up a tablet and brought up the mission report. "Two intelligence operatives, a CIA officer, and a member of MI6. Our information says they are still alive." She looked back at the monitor. "Why?"

"You sent me to clean up a mess. Killing federal officers would have caused a much larger one."

An uncomfortable silence spread throughout the room.

Scorpion cleared her throat. "If there isn't anything else, I need to prep my team for landing."

Dr. Yaras put the tablet back down. "No, Scorpion, that will be all for now."

Scorpion nodded and immediately ended the call.

Dr. Yaras stared at the black screen for a moment, thinking. Then she pressed her remote and brought up Travis's profile again. She finished reading it, then clicked to the next profile.

As she continued, two men rushed inside the command center. One was a Fractal security guard, who ran toward her. "Doctor?" he asked quietly. "We need to speak with you."

Dr. Yaras studied them both. The man next to the security guard was a disheveled little man in a flight uniform, tightly clutching a bag. "Do you now?" she said, looking back to the monitor. She continued to click through profiles.

"Yes, ma'am. It's about the plane. I have the pilot here. He has something to tell you."

That got her to turn back around. She looked directly at the pilot. "You can start with how you lost my plane."

"That's not what happened!" said the pilot, visibly angry. "I didn't lose your plane, it was sabotaged."

"Sabotaged? Hmmm. Hard to prove, given that my plane is at the bottom of the ocean. Convenient for you."

"It was sabotage, and I can prove it." The pilot put his bag down on a nearby table with a metallic thud. Unwrapping it, he revealed the plane's mission computer inside.

"We need to look at the data more," offered the security guard, "but at first glance, the computer does seem to have been tampered with during the flight."

"Interesting." Dr. Yaras stared at the metallic box on the counter. "Do we have any idea who did this?"

"Not yet," said the security guard. "Whoever it was, it's possible they may have died in the crash."

Dr. Yaras turned back to the monitor behind her and began reading through profiles again. "And if not, then that means they are here. On Palmyra."

The security guard slowly nodded. "That is a possibility, ma'am."

"Hmmm. A potential saboteur among us. That should prove very interesting." Dr. Yaras clicked to the next profile.

Will Kirby filled the screen.

"Very interesting indeed."

DID YOU ENJOY THIS EPISODE?

If so, please consider leaving us a review. As an independent author, reviews are vital for getting discovered and finding more readers. Even just a few words could help someone else decide if this book is right for them. We have no fancy publisher or big marketing company behind *Curve of the Dragon*. It's just me.

To make it super easy for you, here's a direct link to review this book:

www.bit.ly/curveonepb

I hope you enjoyed it as much as I did writing it. Thank you for your support!

GET AN EXCLUSIVE FREE BOOK!

If you go to my website and sign up for the mailing list, I will give you a free book that takes place in the *Curve of the Dragon* universe.

That's right. Not a discount. Not a teaser. An entire book. Free! Get it here:

www.seemattwrite.com/mailinglist

It's an exclusive book, you can't buy it anywhere else.

Still not convinced, eh? See the next page for a synopsis:

AUTHOR'S NOTE

First of all, thank you so much for reading this book. As a reader, you have an endless ocean of options out there, and I'm honored you decided to choose mine. I wrote *Curve of the Dragon* because I've always loved spy stories, and I hope you enjoyed reading it as much as I did writing it.

I grew up on stories. Reading them, writing them, watching them, playing them: there's a special magic stories have that can transport us away to exciting adventures in far off locations. But as much as I cherish the books, movies, video games, and comics I grew up on, those were other peoples' stories.

And I really wanted to tell my own.

So I took a chance on myself, and started plotting what would eventually become *Curve of the Dragon*. As a huge fan of spy stories, I wanted to see if I could build one of my own. So I started writing, and kept writing every moment I could. I wrote on lunch breaks and every night after I got home from work. I'd spend every weekend working on outlines or typing out pages. It was slow going, but every week I nudged things forward just a bit more.

In 2019, I got incredibly ill, and was stuck at home for months while I was recovering. Instead of taking it easy, I saw an opportunity to focus on the book, and ultimately pushed through to make what you are now holding in your hands.

Curve of the Dragon ended up not being a traditional novel. It functions more like a TV show, made of smaller episodes that tell a larger story. While there are lots of authors out there writing great spy thriller novels, I only saw one other author writing episodically (hi *Killing Eve*!), and decided I could do something unique with that structure to feel different from a lot of the other series out there. Each episode tells its own smaller story, but they link together and build a larger arc much like a season of a television show. When I realized I could plot out something like a James Bond adventure, but give it the scope of a television season, I got really excited because I hadn't seen that before. And as a fan, that sounded like something I'd want to read.

So that's what I built. *Curve of the Dragon* wears its inspirations on its sleeve, and while there are many spy series I'm quite fond of, James Bond and J.J. Abrams' *Alias* will always be my two favorites. If *Curve* had pop culture parents, it would be them.

I hope you've enjoyed this episode, and look forward to where Will, Maia, and Carter's adventure takes them next!

ACKNOWLEDGMENTS

A small army helped me put this series together, to which I am eternally grateful.

First thank you to my editing team: Jennifer Losi, Lisa Gilliam, and Cheryl Murphy. Without you three, we never would have gotten here. Thank you for your tireless work, and always going above and beyond to help Will and Maia's adventure be as good as it could be. Also, each of you read this more times than anyone should have to read anything. You're all heroes.

Long before the editors saw the manuscript for *Curve*, there were many brave men and women who stepped up to read early drafts as I was working out the story. Thank you to my beta readers: Rachel Rohatgi, Erin Edgington Allison, and Brittany Cox. Thank you for wading through typos and grammar crimes to let me know if the story was working or not. Braver still were my writing group and my alpha readers, who looked at things that might have been *too* early. Thank you

Jennifer Losi, Edward Trybek, C.M. Landrus, Vanessa James Benton, and Peter Holmstrom for reading rough, half finished stuff to see if this was really a story or not.

Through all this, there have been two writers that have been kind enough to mentor me and answer endless barrages of questions. Thank you to both Joshua Hale Fialkov and Marc Guggenheim for not only encouraging me to chase this, but also providing crucial wisdom along the way.

I also want to call out special thanks to Joshua Jones and Ameorry Luo. Josh was my military advisor, and was a huge help with specific details on some of the crazier things that happen on Palmyra. Ameorry was the artist who created all of Maia's investigation boards, and I'm still flabbergasted at just how much content she got in them. Each one is like a little visual overview of the whole story. Also, for those of you kind enough to read the acknowledgements, here's a hint: there's a secret hidden inside the illustrations for Maia's investigation board. If you look at how it grows in each episode, you just might figure it out...

Most of all, thank you to Ed and Jen for all your support. You've always believed this could be something great, even at times when I couldn't see it myself. I consider myself very lucky to call you both family.

And finally, I want to thank you, the reader, for taking a chance on this book. There are a lot of ways you could spend your precious free time, and I'm honored you chose to spend a little with me.

WAIT, WHO WROTE THIS?
ABOUT THE AUTHOR

Matt Stokes grew up on a steady diet of James Bond movies and works with engineers every day, so the only real surprise here is that he didn't combine them sooner.

Curve of the Dragon is his first novel series, but he has previously written on multiple video games, including the WGA-nominated *World in Conflict*. It's his fault the US government blew up the sleepy town of Cascade Falls, WA during Christmas.

When he's not pitching devs crazy plot twists or devising new ways to torture Will Taylor, Matt can be found producing video games. As a producer, he has worked on *Gears of War 4*, *The Evil Within*, *Fallout 4*, *Borderlands 2: Mr. Torgue's Campaign of Carnage* and numerous others.

Matt lives in Los Angeles, California.

For more books and updates, visit:
www.SeeMattWrite.com

twitter.com/seemattwrite

instagram.com/seemattwrite

facebook.com/seemattwrite